THE FLAME
AND THE FLOOD

THE FLAME AND THE FLOOD

Shona Kinsella

www.foxspirit.co.uk

The Flame and The Flood copyright © 2020 Shona Kinsella

Cover Art by Sarah Anne Langton
secretarcticbase.com

Edited by Darren Pulsford

Typesetting and ebook conversion by HandeBooks.co.uk

ISBN: 978-1-910462-30-0

A Fox Spirit Original
Fox Spirit Books
www.foxspirit.co.uk
adele@foxspirit.co.uk

For Charis, Rowan and Seth,
who make my life infinitely more interesting.

One

Talis bowed hir head and sniffed at the sour durafruit. Not ripe. Ze placed it back in the basket and selected another, adding it to hir shopping basket with one pair of hands while paying the trader with the other pair. Ze paused for a moment beneath the canopy of the fruit stall, pulling hir navy blue hair up into a knot on top of hir head, while waiting for a crowd of chattering drones to pass by before stepping out into the thoroughfare. They were boisterous, especially the few winged members of the group, and people moved aside to make way for them.

Talis strolled along in their wake, gaze roaming over the hexagonal marketplace, filled with stalls and people and even a few goats. Ze had already bought meat and vegetables, enough food to keep the boarding house running for the next few days, but ze was enjoying the sun on hir skin and for once, the air was fairly clear, the constant smog from the factories lifting away in the fresh breeze.

Ze wandered over to the stall of the spice merchant to see if there was anything new today. The boat from Akros had come in yesterday, bringing spices, fabrics and alcohol for trade and the market was busy today as a result.

Talis leaned over the spice stall to check the pots at the back and movement caught the corner of hir eye. The edge of the wooden table was sprouting new leaves. Ze looked up sharply, hir antennae quivering. Someone nearby was leaking magic, hir affinity for wood overflowing and causing unintended effects. Talis studied the crowd, seeking out the wielder, searching every face for a clue.

Nothing.

Ze stretched hir antennae, swivelling them around to seek out the vibrations of the magic that was leaking through the market, making the wood behave strangely. A few stalls along, heading in the direction of the boarding house, bark was growing up one of the sanded table legs. Ze set off in that direction, gaze fixed on the stalls and carts of wood. The wielder was close but the number of people here and all of their conflicting vibrations and emotions was making it difficult to focus on hir.

Talis' antennae curled up, and a sour feeling settled in hir stomach. Ze heard Vinhardt a breath later. There was no mistaking the hoarse voice of one of the worst slavers in Cortill; ze had suffered damage to hir throat in a factory accident that left scars on hir neck and on hir voice. Ze was accompanied by the smell of stale beer. Talis wrinkled hir nose up, turning hir face towards the nearest stall as the slaver passed.

What is Vinhardt doing here? This is a mid-level market, this isn't hir hunting ground. I thought they were only taking wielders from the outer reaches.

Talis risked a glance over hir shoulder and saw Vinhardt lingering a few paces away, looking at the goods on a stall on the other side of the thoroughfare. Then it dawned on hir at last. Vinhardt wasn't here as a slaver – ze was just shopping. The slaver might spend time in the inner circles of the colony but ze wasn't one of them. Ze was only a mid-level drone, just like Talis and Almoris.

Cowering between the stall Talis stood at and the next, was a young person. Silver hair fell around a lilac face with eyes screwed shut. Barely more than a larva, ze was shivering despite the mid-morning warmth, hir antennae drooping, both sets of arms wrapped around hir thorax. Beside hir, the wood of the table legs began to bend, causing the stall to sag. Talis' antennae sprang up again. Here was the source of the leak. The affinity wielder.

Talis glanced over hir shoulder at Vinhardt, who was moving away at a leisurely pace. Casually, ze moved along to stand between the two stalls, shielding the wielder with hir body. Hir hand brushed against the small axe that was strapped to hir belt; for a moment ze pictured hirself burying the axe in the slaver's skull but then ze shook hir head. A moment's fantasy, nothing more. Vinhardt laughed at something hir companion said, the sound going through Talis like the factory whistles. Ze suppressed a shudder and feigned interest in the selection of cheeses on the next stall.

'What's this, then?' Vinhardt said, the greed in hir voice clear.

Talis watched from the corner of hir eye as Vinhardt started back towards where ze stood. The wooden tables on either side of the wielder were reshaping themselves as if reaching towards the person who hid between them.

'Go,' Talis hissed.

The wielder opened terrified violet eyes and stared at hir.

'Quickly, run!'

Vinhardt was almost upon them before the wielder leapt to hir feet and took off. Talis pretended to be startled by the sudden movement and fell back against the bowed table. The tortured legs finally gave way, spilling the contents directly into Vinhardt's path. The slaver swore and glared at Talis but was quickly distracted by the sight of the fleeing wielder.

'Stop there!' ze called.

The young person looked over hir shoulder, panic stamped on hir features. Ze took a sharp turn into an alley, skidding on refuse as ze went. Vinhardt kicked pots and dishes out of hir way as ze followed, hir companion lagging behind.

'Keeper of Lost Souls guide hir to safety,' Talis murmured.

Then the stall owner was at hir side, apologising for the collapse, asking if ze was hurt.

'I am well,' Talis said, listening to the sounds of pursuit down the alley. 'Let me help you.'

As quickly as ze could, ze stacked clay pots beside the broken table, picking up cheeses that were wrapped in wax paper and placing them on top of the pots.

'What do you think that was all about?' the trader asked as they worked together to clear the mess. 'A thief perhaps?'

Talis looked up sharply. Could it be that the trader didn't realise what had happened right in front of hir? That a wielder was about to caught and pressed into slavery? Ze sighed and shook hir head. Sometimes it was hard for Talis to remember that the issue which dominated hir whole life was barely considered by others.

'I suppose it must have been something like that,' ze said, standing up and dusting off hir clothing. 'May you have a prosperous day.'

As Talis hurried away the trader was already turning to the next stall and striking up a conversation. No doubt the market would buzz all day with talk of the 'thief' who had been chased off.

The wielder and hir pursuers had been heading east, towards the docks, so Talis headed in that direction through the marketplace and out into the streets beyond, peering into alleys whenever ze could. There was no sign of the wielder or Vinhardt. By the time the factory whistle blew midday, Talis had not located them.

Reluctantly, ze turned for home, the pleasant morning marred by the encounter. The sun no longer felt so good; instead, guilt and helplessness conspired to make hir edgy. If only ze had been able to do more to help the young person. If only ze had come across the wielder sooner, before Vinhardt had appeared in the market.

Talis looked up from hir thoughts, startled, when someone touched hir elbow. Batanel had appeared at hir side. If Talis had not been so absorbed in hir thoughts, ze would have picked up on Batanel's familiar vibrations before hir friend had been close enough to touch hir.

'Almoris sent me out looking for you,' Batanel said. 'There's been a bit of excitement around the boarding house.'

'What's happened?' Talis asked, alarm making hir hearts beat faster, a syncopated rhythm that thrummed in hir thorax. 'Is ze alright?'

'Almoris is fine. Vinhardt was searching the alleys around the house, shouting about a wood-wielder.'

Talis frowned. Was it just a coincidence that the conflict ze had seen in the market had continued around the boarding house? 'What is Almoris doing now?' ze asked, picking up hir pace.

'We waited until Vinhardt had gone and then Almoris went out to search the alleys in case the wielder that Vinhardt was looking for is hiding nearby. Ze asked me to find you and bring you home in case the wielder is hurt.'

'Soot and ashes,' Talis muttered.

'What's wrong?' Batanel asked.

'I saw a wood-wielder in the market, leaking all over the place,' Talis said, picking up the pace. 'Vinhardt spotted hir before I could do anything to get hir away. They took off down an alley and I tried to follow on parallel streets, but I lost them.'

'You think it's the same wielder?'

'That seems likely. I don't like Vinhardt being so close to the boarding house.'

They hurried through the streets, side-by-side, skirting around large drones who watched them go. As they passed the textile factory, a stream of smaller workers in patched and ragged clothes made their way inside. Talis grimaced at the cruel irony, hir anger at the greed of the factory owners never far away.

They rounded the corner at the end of the factory and almost walked straight into a large crick, pulling a carriage. Batanel jumped back, pulling Talis with hir. The carriage driver cursed at them, cracking the whip next to the crick's ear, driving it on. A curtain covered the window in the carriage door, and it twitched as it drew level with them, revealing a hand that glittered with jewellery before the curtain fell back again and the carriage continued on its way.

Talis leaned against a soot-stained wall, waiting for hir hearts to slow. Batanel's green skin had paled and ze was breathing fast.

'I hate the overseers,' Batanel grunted. 'They act as if the streets belong to them as well as the factories.'

'Let's go,' Talis said, squeezing Batanel's forearm.

'Almoris?' Talis called as soon as ze was through the boarding house door. 'Are you here?' The hexagonal hallway stretched before hir, dust motes dancing in a beam of light. The water-clock gurgled and Talis realised that ze was leaking a little hirself, the stress of the morning wearing down hir control. Ze was glad that none of the boarders were home at this time of day.

'In the kitchen,' Almoris called, sounding cheerful.

Breathing a sigh of relief, Talis strode to the back of the building, Batanel close at hir back. The scent of the morning's meal lingered in the air and Talis noted a dirty mark on the floor as ze passed.

'Is everything alright?' ze asked, walking into the kitchen.

As soon as ze entered the room, ze stopped in hir tracks. Sitting at the kitchen table was the wielder from earlier. Hir silver hair was dishevelled, tunic and leggings covered in dirt. Hir hands were wrapped around a cup of hot broth, the steam tugging at Talis' attention. Thankfully, the wielder's affinity was no longer leaking; Talis' table was unaffected.

The wielder's jaw dropped. 'You! You were in the market!' Ze got to hir feet and backed away from the table.

Talis slowly placed hir shopping basket on the table and held all four hands up, palms towards the young person and Batanel did the same at hir side. Hir antennae were quivering in sympathy to the young wielder's fear.

'Don't be alarmed,' Talis said. 'We're not going to hurt you.'

'Why should I believe you?' the wielder asked, back pressed against the wall, eyes wide and frightened. Hir antennae stood rigid, and Talis felt hir own spring up in response.

Talis looked towards the deep sink at the other end of the room and waited until ze knew the wielder was looking too. Then ze stretched out a hand and made a beckoning gesture. A stream of water rose into the air above the sink, forming a ball which floated towards Talis. Ze moved hir fingers as if plucking the strings of a harp and the water began to dance, splitting and flowing in sinuous shapes.

The wielder watched, eyes shining.

Talis directed the water into a cup that sat on the table. 'What's your name?'

'Juki,' the wielder said. Then, in a quieter voice, 'You already know I have an affinity for wood.'

Almoris stepped towards Juki. 'You can relax. You're safe here.' Ze gestured to the seat that Juki had recently vacated. 'Please, finish your broth.'

'How did you get away from Vinhardt?' Talis asked, as Juki slid into the seat again. Talis was still suspicious but the predominant feeling that came from the wielder was fear so ze was willing to hear hir out.

Juki met Talis's gaze as ze spoke and gave no signs of deception. 'I came out beside the textile factory. There was a carriage stopped outside, the driver was dozing on top, so I slid underneath and hid. I heard them come out of the alley, and I curled up as tight as I could. The slaver was so angry, it made my antennae shrink. Ze was shouting and the carriage driver woke up. Ze didn't want to admit to being asleep so ze swore I hadn't come that way.'

'How did you come to be *here*?' Talis asked, looking at hir spouse.

'I stayed under the carriage until I couldn't hear them anymore. I was so scared, I wanted to just stay there all day, but my affinity was still leaking a little. The wood floor of the carriage started to look like it had been carved and I worried that the driver would notice something, so I crept out and ran. I took the first alley I came to and I was sneaking along when Almoris found me. Ze said I could hide here until it was safe.' Juki looked back and forward between Almoris and Talis, clearly reluctant to get hir saviour into trouble.

'I heard Vinhardt shouting and searching in the street.' Almoris said. 'As soon as ze and hir companion moved on, I went looking for Juki here. I could feel hir affinity as soon as I turned into the alley ze was in. It was just luck that Vinhardt didn't stumble over hir.'

'Very well,' Talis said, sitting down with a sigh. It all sounded reasonable. Perhaps it really was just a coincidence that the conflict ze had seen begin at the market should end so close to hir home. 'Batanel, would you take Juki upstairs? The attic room is empty.'

'Of course,' Batanel answered from hir place by the door.

'Juki, there is a wardrobe full of clothes, I'm sure you'll be able to find something that fits. I'll warm some water, so you can wash up. Almoris and I have work to do this afternoon. I'll bring a meal up to you later and we can decide what to do next.'

Two

When they were alone in the kitchen, Talis pulled out the meat that ze had bought at the market and began to cut it up with sharp, tense movements, while Almoris unpacked the vegetables and began chopping at hir side. Talis lifted a heavy pot onto the table and set it down with a thump before tossing some of the meat in.

'What's bothering you?' Almoris asked, leaning against the table.

Talis sighed. 'I don't like that they were so close to our home.'

'You said yourself the chase started in the market. It's just luck that they came in this direction.'

'Well, whose luck?' Talis paused in hir work. 'Juki's? Ours? Vinhardt's?'

Almoris tensed, crossing hir arms across hir chest. 'I wasn't seen, Talis. This isn't my first shift.'

Talis bowed hir head in apology. 'I know, my love. I just … Vinhardt is the worst of them. Ze makes my skin crawl.'

Almoris leaned in and Talis wrapped hir arms around hir spouse, one pair stroking Almoris' hair while the other pair held hir tight.

'If we're only going to help people when there's no danger then we're in the wrong business,' Almoris said, hir breath warm against Talis' chest.

'I know.' Talis rested hir head on top of hir spouse's, careful to avoid Almoris' antennae. 'Ever since you were attacked last moon, I've been so worried that something could happen to you. I can't … I can't live with the thought of spending my days without you.'

Almoris sighed. 'I was careless. I was outside of the colony, travelling alone, at night. I practically invited bandits to try and rob me. Nothing like that will happen again. No lasting harm was done.'

'You were wounded. I could have lost you.' Even the thought made Talis feel panicky and hir antennae started to tremble.

'The wound has healed, my love. And I have promised you that I will be more careful.' Almoris rubbed hir head against Talis' chest, releasing hir own secret scent, marking Talis as belonging to hir.

Talis breathed deeply, inhaling Almoris' scent, feeling hirself relax. Home. Peace. Safety. All of these existed in this moment, within hir spouse's embrace. Reluctantly, ze pulled away and turned back to the meat, which wouldn't prepare itself.

'Juki can stay here for a few days,' ze said, 'until we're sure it's safe. Then we can see about getting hir out of Slyvo.'

Batanel poked hir head through the door. 'Can I come in?'

'Of course,' Almoris said, adding wood to the fire and making a quick gesture, causing the flames to leap up. Ze hauled the heavy pot stand over and positioned it carefully.

'Is our newest guest settled?' Talis asked.

'Ze is,' Batanel answered, coming into the room and letting the door close behind hir. 'Have you thought about what to do with hir yet?'

'Let things die down for a few days and then figure it out,' Talis said, scooping up the rest of the meat and tossing it into the pot with some spices and water. 'Maybe reach out to Milane in Whillet, see if we can send hir there.'

'The Akrian ship is scheduled to leave at the end of the week,' Batanel said. 'Nyqam may be able to get hir on board.'

Talis and Almoris exchanged a look. For years, they had been using the same few contacts to smuggle people out of Cortill and, eventually, out of Slyvo altogether. Other colonies in other countries had a more enlightened view of affinity wielders. And of the poor.

Half a year ago, they had met Batanel, who had been a sailor before settling in Cortill. Ze had friends and contacts all over the world and had opened up new possibilities for getting wielders to safety.

'Great idea,' Almoris said, hoisting the pot over the fire and placing a bucket of water in front of Talis.

The water-wielder dipped hir hands into the cool water and concentrated on heat. Ze thought of fire and sunshine and warm blankets and the water warmed at hir prompting.

'Do you mind taking this up to Juki while we finish getting the evening meal prepared?'

'Of course.' Batanel took the bucket and headed for the door. 'I will go looking for Nyqam tonight. I know which tavern ze likes best. I should be able to find hir there after dark.'

After the evening meal had been served and the boarders had retired to their rooms or gone out for the evening, Talis climbed the steep, cramped stairs to the attic room. The heat up here was oppressive and ze felt sorry for the wood-wielder. Most of the people staying in the house were legitimate boarders, factory and dock workers who, for various reasons, preferred not to keep their own home. This provided an income for the bonded pair as well as cover for the other activities that Talis, Almoris and Batanel were involved with. Apart from the fact that it was normal for many people to come and go from the house, the presence of all of the non-wielders helped to mask the vibrations that their affinities gave off.

Unfortunately for Juki, it meant that it was safest if ze stayed in hir room while the others were home.

Talis knocked, relieved to see that the wooden door looked normal. Juki seemed to have stopped leaking for the moment. They would have to pay attention though – if wood started behaving strangely around the house, it would only be a matter of time before one of the boarders noticed and there was a hefty reward for providing Vinhardt with information about wielders.

'Come in,' Juki called from inside.

Talis stepped into the room, holding out a tray with food. 'I brought you a meal.'

'Thank you,' Juki said. 'Not just for the food. For helping me.'

The young wielder had cleaned up and changed into a long, flowing robe of shimmering blue silk. Ze looked almost like a different person.

'May I?' Talis indicated one of the stools next to a low table, where ze placed the tray.

'Of course!' Juki sat down and looked hungrily at the stew and bread in front of hir.

'May we talk while you eat?' Talis carefully examined the wood of the stool before sitting on it. You could never be too careful with a leaking wielder around. It made their magic unpredictable.

Juki nodded and picked up the bread, tearing it in half.

'How long have you known you were a wielder?' Talis asked, crossing one pair of arms and resting the others on the table.

'About two years,' Juki mumbled around a mouthful of food. 'My nest-guardian threw me out when I started to leak. Said I would put them all at risk if I stayed.'

Talis shook hir head. Too many of the wielders they helped shared such stories. 'You did well to avoid the slave gangs for so long.'

'I've had a few close calls. For a while I stayed with a group, in an abandoned warehouse, in the north quadrant. But then Hyphil was taken. After that we all sort of drifted apart.' Juki looked sad. Talis leaned forward, wanting to offer some comfort but the young wielder shook hirself and sat up straighter. 'Anyway, that was that. I've been on my own since then. It's easier that way.'

'Were you close to Hyphil?'

'Not as close as I was with Lessin, Hyphil's sibling. Ze had actually been a slave in a button factory but ze escaped when there was a fire.' Juki's face took on a haunted expression and this time, Talis did lean forward and place a hand on the young wielder's arm.

'Ze must have been very brave.'

'Ze was. Lessin was covered in scars from hir time in the factory. Ze was a wood-wielder, like me. They made hir power the windmill, all by hirself. When ze got tired and let the blades slow, they would beat hir. Burn hir.' Tears slipped down Juki's cheeks. 'Ze worked eighteen hours a day, all so they would have more power for their machines. After Hyphil was taken, Lessin and I were together for a while, until we were cornered by a gang of slavers one day. Ze couldn't face going back.'

'You don't need to tell me,' Talis said softly.

'Ze threw hirself through a window. The glass shattered …
it was a quick ending.'

'I'm so sorry, Juki.'

The young wood-wielder scrubbed at hir eyes and shook
hir head. 'It was a long time ago.'

'Do you know how to stop your affinity leaking?' Talis
asked, trying to steer the conversation on to less painful
ground.

'Stop it? Is that even possible?'

'Of course. I can teach you if you like.'

'What do I have to do?' Juki pushed the spoon around the
half-eaten bowl of stew.

'All you have to do is use it.'

Juki cocked hir head, one antenna raised inquisitively. 'Use
what?'

'Your affinity. Use your power over wood, stop it building
up until it leaks.'

'Like you did with the water?' Juki frowned.

'Indeed,' Talis said, resting hir chin in a hand.

'But … you could be caught!'

'True. But if you don't use it, the affinity *will* leak from
you, uncontrolled, and sooner or later you will certainly be
caught. By learning to use your affinity, to wield it, you can
control it, only let it out when you are safe and unobserved.'

Juki's antennae quivered. 'I'm scared of it,' ze said in a low
voice. 'All it's ever done is cause me trouble.'

'I understand.' Talis placed one of hir hands over Juki's.
'You do not have to learn. We are looking for a way to get you
away from here, to somewhere that wielders are not enslaved
as they are here. You will be free to use your affinity or not, as
you wish. But should you decide to keep it hidden, this is the
only way I know to do so.'

Juki bowed hir head. 'I will think on it.' The young person
used the bread to soak up the last of the stew from hir bowl.
'Where will you send me?'

'We're not sending you, Juki. You are free to go or not.
We're just arranging the possibility for you.'

Juki looked sceptical.

'We may be able to arrange passage to Akros, should that
interest you.'

'I have heard tales of Akros,' Juki said, hir tone filled with awe. 'It is said that they have no factories there. That their leaders have forbidden it. Is that true?'

'To the best of my knowledge it is true,' Talis confirmed. 'Goods are still made by small businesses. And all wielders may use their affinity to create and offer their creations for sale.'

'Don't the seed classes object to that?'

'There are no classes in Akros.'

Juki looked startled and Talis suppressed a chuckle. Ze had felt the same confusion when ze first learned that the classes weren't universal, that other countries were not like Slyvo.

'I wouldn't know what to do there,' Juki said softly.

Talis reached into hir pocket and pulled out a small chunk of wood. 'I'll leave you to think it over,' ze said.

Batanel did not appear until late the next morning, after breakfast had been served and cleared away and most of the boarders had left for their various places of employment.

'Where have you been?' Almoris asked, looking up from the loom on which ze was weaving cloth in intricate patterns.

'It took a while to track down Nyqam, and then ze wanted me to play cards with hir all night.' Batanel yawned. 'On the plus side, we won quite a lot of money, which put Nyqam in a very good mood.'

'A good enough mood to help us?' Talis asked, stepping out of the front room.

'Yes. Ze is willing to transport Juki to Akros and see that ze has accommodation. Then, our young wielder will be on hir own.'

'Will there be problems with the sailors?' Almoris asked.

Batanel chuckled. 'It seems that Akrian sailors consider it good luck to have a wood-wielder on board, in case of storms. They already have one traveling with them but they're happy to make room for one more.'

Talis frowned, wondering what wood had to do with storms. Then it came to hir. A skilled wood-wielder may well be able to keep a stricken boat afloat and bring it in to shore safely. Hir mind's eye saw a wooden ship battling all the power of the sea, surrounded by enormous swells of water, and Juki standing mid-deck, holding the ship together by force of will. Then ze remembered the way the young wielder flinched away from hir ability.

'Let us hope they have smooth sailing, all the way to Akros,' ze said.

Batanel went upstairs and Talis returned to the front room, where ze was repairing a pair of work-boots for one of the dockworkers who boarded with them. The wooden sole had cracked and Talis had removed it and crafted a new sole. Ze thought how much easier the task would be if ze wielded wood rather than water then snorted. This task would be easier but fetching water from the well out back would be much harder.

Talis carefully applied glue to the leather bottom of the boot and pressed it to the new wooden sole. While ze held the pieces together, waiting for the glue to set, hir antennae quivered.

Something wasn't right.

Ze looked around the room, seeking the source of hir discomfort. The sensation grew stronger and a familiar sour feeling settled into hir stomach.

Talis' hearts dropped. It took all hir control to carefully set the boot down, rather than just dropping it and running for the back of the house.

Vinhardt was outside.

The slaver was standing at the door to the house across the street, talking with the nest-guardian who lived there.

'Almoris, come here,' Talis called in a low voice.

Almoris poked hir head around the doorway. 'What is it?'

Talis nodded to the window.

'Soot and ashes. What's ze doing here?'

'Looking for Juki?' Talis suggested.

As they watched, an egg cart came down the street and paused in front of the boarding house, obscuring their view.

'Please, go upstairs and make sure our guest remains hidden,' Talis said.

Almoris hurried away just as the cart moved to reveal Vinhardt walking towards the front door.

Talis turned away from the window and quickly massaged hir antennae, a self-soothing technique that never failed to calm hir. Ze straightened hir tunic just as a loud knock came from the door. Glancing up the stairs on the way past to the door, ze hoped that none of the boarders that were still here would choose that moment to come downstairs.

Please don't recognise me from the market ze thought as ze opened the door.

'I'm sorry, we don't have any rooms available at the moment,' Talis said before Vinhardt had a chance to speak.

'What?' Vinhardt said, stepping back.

'Aren't you looking for a room?'

'Of course not!' the slaver spluttered, spreading hir iridescent wings. 'Don't you know who I am?'

Talis kept a carefully crafted blank expression on hir face. 'Should I?'

'Never mind,' Vinhardt muttered, clearly knocked off hir stride. 'I'm looking for a vagrant. Ran away from hir nest a few days ago.'

'That's terrible,' Talis said, clenching hir teeth at the sheer brashness of the lie.

'Young, lilac skin, silver hair. Have you seen anyone like that?'

'Not that I can recall,' Talis said. 'There *was* a young person around yesterday but hir skin was grey, not lilac, and I'm sure ze had dark hair. Although ... maybe ... I'm not so sure now. Ze was covered in soot...'

'Where did you see hir?' Vinhardt asked, an edge to hir voice.

'In the alley round back. Ze was filthy and I chased hir away,' Talis feigned a look of disgust. 'We don't need that sort round here – obviously from the outer edges of the colony. This is a good mid-area.'

'Did you see which direction ze went in?'

'Out towards the geriatric zone.'

Vinhardt was backing away almost before Talis had finished speaking.

'Good luck,' Talis said before closing the door and leaning against it. Vinhardt would waste time searching the geriatric zone, speaking to people whose memories were fading. Ze wouldn't be able to be quite sure whether they were remembering yesterday or last year.

Talis forced hirself to wait a full five minutes before ze went upstairs. A delayed sense of panic hit hir on the way up the steep stairs to the attic room and ze sat down heavily.

'Talis?' Almoris opened the attic room door. 'Is everything well?'

'Yes,' Talis answered, rubbing hir antennae. 'Yes, it just caught up with me. Vinhardt is gone.'

Almoris ducked back into the attic room, returning a moment later with a dusty Juki by hir side.

'I hope you weren't too frightened,' Talis said to the young wielder.

'Only a little,' Juki answered. 'When Almoris closed the panel and I was tucked away in the eaves it felt safe and scary all at once. Does that make sense?'

'It does.' Talis got to hir feet. 'With Vinhardt asking about you around here, it's even more important that you stay out of sight.'

Over the next few days, Juki stayed hidden in the attic room. In the evenings, Almoris and Talis took turns spending time with the young wielder, learning more about hir, chatting about hir dreams for a new life.

Three days after Juki had arrived in their lives, Talis sat in the attic room, carving a delicate wand of ash; a gift for Almoris that ze had been working on for almost a full season. Ze sat quietly by the fire, working the wood slowly and gently, while Juki sat at hir feet, watching raptly.

'Have you ever been to Akros?' Juki asked, head resting on hir knees.

'No, I've never been out of Cortill,' Talis answered. 'Batanel has been all over the place though. You could ask hir about Akros.'

Juki shook hir head and hir antennae curled up, close to hir head.

'What's wrong?' Talis asked, frowning. Ze could feel the bitter tang of fear from the young wood-wielder.

At first, Juki just squeezed hirself into a tight little ball and Talis thought that ze wouldn't answer. Juki wrapped one set of arms around hir legs and the other over hir head, hiding hir face.

'I don't think Batanel likes me very much.' Hir voice came out muffled.

'Why?'

'Ze's so solemn. Ze never smiles.'

'I've never seen Batanel to be anything other than kind and gentle. I once saw hir rescue a baby mud-popper from a patch of suck-mud it had gotten stuck in. Ze kept it in a box in hir room for almost a whole moon, until it was big enough and strong enough to fend for itself.' Talis smiled fondly at the memory. 'Ze can be reserved but ze has a gentle heart.'

'A mud-popper?' Juki said with a surprised laugh. 'They're ugly little things.'

'This is true,' Talis sighed. 'And even the lovely trilling sound they make grows wearisome when it's keeping you up at night. But Batanel can never turn hir back on an orphan.'

Juki cocked hir head to the side as if in thought, hir body relaxing a little. Talis watched the young wielder from the corner of hir eye while frowning at the wand. 'Oh, soot and ashes,' ze cursed, dropping the wand into hir lap.

'What's wrong?' Juki asked.

'No matter how I try, I just can't get the curve of this vine right,' Talis answered, frustration making hir voice tight. 'This is the third wand I've tried; you'd think I would be getting better at this. But no. The vine still looks clumsy.'

'May I see it?'

Talis held the wand out to the wood-wielder, trying to hide the flare of satisfaction ze felt. Ze had to concentrate on keeping hir antennae low and despondent looking.

Juki was holding the wand towards the fire, letting the light from the flames play across the wood. 'I don't see anything wrong… ah, just below the rose, where the vine curves round towards the key, is that the bit?'

'That's it.' Talis tipped hir head back and closed hir eyes most of the way. Ze left them open just a slit so that ze could watch Juki. Ze was quite sure ze knew what was going to happen next.

'I can feel it … the wood *wants* to curve delicately. It just needs…' Juki trailed off, totally focussed on the wand now.

Talis' antennae vibrated and the hair at the back of hir legs rose in response to the building power in the small room. Ze braced hirself, taking most of hir weight off the chair and onto the powerful muscles in hir legs, just in case Juki lost control and the wooden chair suffered for it.

'There!' Juki looked up, eyes shining in triumph. 'I did it!'

Talis smiled and accepted the wand when Juki held it out to hir. The vine now curved gracefully down the length of the wand, delicate leaves and shoots extending to the sides.

Three

Talis stared out the window at the rapidly darkening street. The sky had been overcast all day; thick, heavy rain clouds trapping the smoke that pumped endlessly from the factories to wind and snake through the streets. About an hour ago, the rain had started to fall, offering a mixed blessing. On the one hand, it gave Juki an excuse to wear a cloak and hood. It was also likely that fewer people would be on the streets and most of those would have their heads down. On the other hand, it meant they couldn't risk using ash to darken Juki's hair and skin as they had planned in case it started to wash off.

Talis sighed and rubbed hir antennae, turning to the doorway as Almoris entered the front room, Batanel a step behind.

'Are we ready?' Almoris asked.

'As ready as we're going to be,' Talis answered. 'Where's Juki?'

'I'm here,' the young wielder said, stepping into the room. Ze looked at Talis shyly. 'I have something for you.'

'You don't need to give me anything,' Talis said, half frowning and half smiling.

'I know. But I wanted to.' Juki held out a small wooden statue, and Talis took it, holding it up to the light from the paraffin lamp on the wall.

'Is this … is it me?' Talis asked in wonder.

Juki nodded. 'I hope you don't mind.'

Talis studied the intricately detailed figure. It showed perfectly the shape of hir eyes, the way hir shoulder-length hair flicked out, how delicate hir antennae were, while also hinting at the strength in hir limbs and giving the suggestion of movement. 'It's beautiful,' ze said, running hir thumb over the tiny antennae on top of the statue's head. 'I don't know how to thank you.'

'I never would have tried something like this if it hadn't been for you. It seemed fitting that the first thing I made should be a gift for you.'

Talis carefully placed the statue on a low table. Perhaps there was more strength in Juki than ze had originally thought. To have created something so accomplished in such a short time was very impressive indeed. Maybe the young wood-wielder would bring luck to the Akian sailors after all.

The evening whistle blew, setting Talis's teeth on edge.

'It's time,' said Almoris, wrapping a cloak around Juki's shoulders.

'Be careful out there,' Talis said to the young wielder. 'Do exactly what Batanel says and keep your wits about you.'

Juki looked doubtfully at Batanel. 'I would feel so much better if you were coming with me,' ze said to Talis.

'The person you're meeting is expecting Batanel; it has to be hir. You'll be fine.'

'Couldn't you come too?'

'We don't have time for this,' Batanel said, a little grumpily. 'Nyqam will not wait for us.'

Talis looked from Juki to Almoris and back again. 'Very well, I'll come too.'

'Then so will I,' Almoris said firmly, causing the flames on the candles around the room to flare.

'The boarders will be returning soon – one of us should be here,' Talis said.

'I'll leave a note.'

'If we stand around discussing this much longer, they'll be back before we leave, and Juki will be exposed.' Batanel definitely sounded annoyed this time.

'Let's go.' Talis strode across the room and the others followed.

Almoris scrawled a quick note to the boarders while Talis fetched their cloaks, then they all hurried outside. Batanel took the lead, with Talis and Juki walking side by side and Almoris bringing up the rear. The street was getting busier now, with workers from the factories making their way home and to the taverns that were dotted around the colony streets, in higher concentration closest to the factories. Talis wondered not for the first time, why such establishments were so often located where the people could least afford to frequent them.

Juki bumped into Talis and the water-wielder used the

opportunity to stage a fake stumble, giving hir an unobtrusive way to look behind them, checking for signs that they were being followed. No-one seemed to be taking any notice of them. Ze straightened up and flashed Juki a quick smile.

They walked mostly in silence, each locked in their own thoughts. Talis could feel the fear coming from Juki but ze also knew that words would offer no comfort. Ze wondered how different hir life would have been if ze had been offered the opportunity to escape at such a young age. Could ze have gone to Akros or somewhere else like it and been free? But then, ze would have never met Almoris. And ze had freedom of a sort. Certainly, more than the wielders that were taken as slaves to work in the mills and factories, forced to use their gift for the benefit of others. If they had been born poor, anyway. Rich wielders were allowed to practice their art openly, even make a living from it. They became renowned as leaders in their craft, while they're affinity siblings were worked to death more often than not.

Talis ground hir teeth at the injustice of it all. Ze was almost walking up Batanel's back before ze realised that ze had started walking faster in hir anger. Juki was still at hir side, scurrying to keep up.

'Sorry,' Talis said, dropping back with a sheepish glance at the young wood-wielder.

'Are you well?' Juki asked, voice high-pitched and tight.

Look at hir, Talis thought. *Ze's frightened, about to leave the only home ze's ever known and still, ze has concern for me.* 'I'm fine,' ze answered, forcing a smile. 'I got caught up in my thoughts. More importantly, are *you* well?'

Juki ducked hir head in an ambivalent gesture. 'I'm scared but also hopeful.'

Talis reached out and squeezed Juki's hand then glanced over hir shoulder. Almoris was still behind them, scanning the street for anyone taking too much notice of them.

Up ahead, Batanel turned into a tavern that spilled warm light onto the grey stones that paved the street. When Talis opened the door for Juki, they were met by a wall of sound and the smell of freshly baked bread. Batanel was making hir way across the room to a small table at the back. Soon all four of them were gathered around the table with drinks of warm nectar in front of them.

Juki sat in the corner, tucked into the shadows, head bent over the table. 'What are we doing?' ze asked in a low voice.

'Throwing off suspicion,' Batanel said into hir cup. 'It is not common to see us all leaving the boarding house in the evening and travelling to the docks. Anyone who was paying attention may wonder what we were doing, might think to tell Vinhardt about it the next time ze comes sniffing around. However, there's nothing unusual about a few of us from the boarding house taking a drink together of an evening.'

'But what about the docks?'

'Don't worry,' Talis said. 'We'll get you there in time.'

'We've been doing this for a long time,' Almoris said gently. 'We know what we're doing.'

Juki's feet tapped a nervous rhythm on the floor as the others drank and put on a show of laughing and chatting. An ornate water clock stood in one corner of the warm tavern and Talis glanced at it frequently. When quarter of an hour had passed with no sign of anyone taking any undue notice of them, ze knew it was probably safe to move to the next stage of the plan.

'Let's go,' Talis said, draining hir cup and pushing it into the middle of the table.

The four of them got to their feet and Juki made to walk across the room and back out the door they had come in. Talis took the wood-wielder's elbow and turned hir back, towards a small door half concealed by a heavy curtain.

The door led to a short hexagonal corridor and then out into a courtyard with a water pump and some chickens in a coop. Talis chuckled as Juki looked around in wonder. In the corner of the courtyard was a gate, the only way out.

Juki was the first to reach it. Ze pulled the handle only to discover it was locked.

'What do we do now?' ze said over hir shoulder. 'I might be able to open it, but they'll know someone was here.'

'There's no need.' Batanel held up a black iron key. 'Like Almoris said; we've done this before.'

On the other side of the gate they found themselves in a narrow alley lined with more gates. They walked towards the far end and at the third gate on the other side of the alley,

Batanel halted them. Ze passed a hand over the key and its shape changed.

Juki gasped. 'You have an affinity for iron!'

Batanel grinned, hir teeth glowing faintly in the dark alley. Ze unlocked the gate and held it while the others passed through into a much smaller courtyard than the one behind the tavern. The metallic tang of blood hung heavy in the air.

Talis's antennae were taut, seeking out any threat towards them.

'Where are we?' Juki asked, voice trembling.

'Behind a butcher's store,' Talis answered. 'There's nothing to fear.'

Batanel stood beside the door leading into the store and once more passed a hand over the key, shaping it to match the lock.

Batanel's skill has certainly made new routes possible for us, Talis thought as the iron-wielder opened the door into the small workspace. Despite the smell, the counters and floor were spotless, well-cared-for aprons hung on the wall and all of the butcher's tools were neatly stored.

To the left of the room was a latched door which led to the cold storage room. A slate hung on the outside of the door, listing the contents. Talis glanced down the list then took a few steps over to the window that looked out onto the street. The buildings here were all workshops, closed and empty for the night.

'It's clear,' Talis said.

Batanel once more transformed hir key and the group slipped out, quickly crossing the cobbled street and heading into another alley.

'We'll be at Nyqam's room soon,' Batanel said, speaking over hir shoulder. 'Ze won't be expecting so many of us, so it's probably best if I go in first and explain. We don't want to alarm hir.'

'What happens when we get there?' Juki asked.

'Nyqam will sneak you onto the boat during the night and you'll hide where the customs officers won't find you. Once you've left port, Nyqam will let you out and you'll be on your way to freedom and happiness.' Batanel looked back and smiled. 'I envy you a little.'

'Why do you stay here?' Juki asked.

Batanel spread all four arms, taking in the alley and all of its squalor. 'And miss all this?'

Talis snorted a laugh.

'Some must stay in Cortill and other colonies throughout Slyvo to help other wielders escape.' Batanel's expression had turned serious. 'One day though, I too will leave this place and make a better life somewhere else.'

They turned into a narrow street, scarcely wider than the alley they had just left, empty crates and lobster pots stacked at either side. The street-lamps were of the oil variety, not the newer gas lamps that were used in the wealthier parts of the colony. Pools of light lay on the wet cobbles and the tang of salt filled the air, replacing the scent of soot that lay over the streets around the factories. At regular intervals, metal staircases climbed the outside of the buildings, to upper story rooms.

The buildings here were hexagonal and built three stories high. Alternate buildings were set back from the street with small strips of ground in front of them. Many of the residents used this space to grow thistles to supplement their diets. The docks were only just considered a mid-area; the people there scrabbling to stay out of the outer reaches of the colony where life was even harder, and all were prey to people like Vinhardt.

'Nyqam's room is up there,' Batanel said, drawing to a halt and pointing to a staircase ahead. 'Wait here and I'll wave when it's safe.'

Talis scanned the street. Some of the windows showed signs of occupation in the rooms beyond but overall, the place had a deserted feel to it. The building they had stopped beside appeared to be empty and Juki leaned back against the wall as they watched Batanel climb the staircase and enter Nyqam's room.

Talis fought the urge to pace; ze had never been very good at waiting. Instead, ze began to count silently, marking off the time until Batanel came back. Ze looked at Juki and realised ze would miss the young wielder, a fact that surprised hir. Talis had been doing this long enough to have stopped getting attached to the people they helped, but something about

Juki had gotten under hir skin. Ze thought of the little statue. *Maybe that's what made the difference.*

Almoris moved restlessly at hir side, peering up at the door to Nyqam's room.

What's taking so long?

Talis had almost decided to go up and see what was happening when Juki stiffened, clutching Almoris' arm.

'Is that Vinhardt?' the wood wielder squeaked, pointing down the street to where a stocky figure was walking towards them, flanked by two other people.

'I think so,' Talis answered, gripping Juki's arm. 'Let's go.'

The three of them began to walk back in the direction they had come from, quickly but without running.

'Soot and ashes,' Almoris swore as three more shapes appeared in the drizzle up ahead. 'We'll have to make a run for it. Use the alleys. Head for the tavern we were in earlier. I'm not much larger than Juki, I'll try to lead them away.'

'Take care, my love.' Talis squeezed Almoris' hand.

As they passed the mouth of an alley, Almoris nodded. 'Go,' ze hissed, giving Juki a push towards Talis and breaking in the opposite direction.

'Hey!' A shout sounded behind them followed by the echoing clop of wooden-soled boots on cobbles.

Talis grabbed Juki's hand and pulled the young wielder along in hir wake. The alleys were dark and narrow and full of obstacles – not ideal for racing along in the dark and the rain. Talis stepped in something that squished and hir foot slid along the cobbles, almost tipping hir. Juki grabbed hir arm, steadying hir, and they ran on, footsteps bouncing off the buildings around them, making it sound like there was a whole army in pursuit.

Talis reached out with hir affinity and mentally touched the water that filled the air around them in the form of rain. Ze threw the rain behind them with unnatural force, obscuring the view of whoever followed, while simultaneously slicking the cobbles with water, making the footing even more treacherous.

Controlling water in so many tiny droplets required immense effort; Talis knew ze wouldn't be able to keep it up for long, especially while running flat out. They had to find somewhere to hide. As if Juki had read hir mind, the young wielder pulled hir into an alley to the left and then the next on the right.

'Blasted furnace,' Talis muttered, realising they had run into a dead end.

If they turned back, they would run right into their pursuers. One side of the alley was bounded by buildings but the other had walls leading onto courtyards and outdoor work areas.

'Quick, over the wall,' Talis hissed, wishing that Batanel was here with hir key. Ze bent down and boosted Juki up to the top of the wall before taking a few steps back and running at the wall, leaping up and grabbing for the top. Ze missed.

Juki slid down the other side of the wall as Talis tried again. The water-wielder still couldn't quite get a hold of the top.

'Talis, hurry,' Juki called over the wall.

Ze sounds terrified.

'Did you really think you could get away from me?'

Talis whirled at the sound of Vinhardt's distinctive voice. The mouth of the alley was empty.

'You're coming with me,' Vinhardt said, just as Talis realised the voice was coming from the other side of the wall.

Juki screamed and Talis threw hirself at the top of the wall again, hir hands failing to find enough purchase to pull hirself up.

'Let me go,' Juki sobbed.

Talis jumped again and managed to grab a hold of the top of the wall. Ze strained with all hir might, arm and shoulder muscles burning, but hir bulk was more than ze could lift under these conditions. Ze wedged hir feet into a crack between the rough stones that made up the wall and clung there, searching out another foothold so that ze could scale the wall.

Juki cried harder and then there was the hard crack of a slap on bare skin. Talis's feet slipped and ze fell off the wall. Bile rose in hir throat. There was nothing ze could do but listen to Vinhardt dragging Juki away.

Four

Talis trudged dejectedly back towards the place ze had last seen Almoris, head down and shoulders slumped. *Keeper of Lost Souls, please keep Almoris safe. Guide my feet back to my spouse. And take care of Juki.*

Ze could still hear the young wielder's wails echoing in hir mind. If only ze hadn't sent Juki over the wall first. How had the slavers managed to get around there so quickly? Was it just coincidence that they had been found tonight?

Talis didn't think so.

Ze reached the street where they had separated and began peering into alleys on the other side, antennae standing straight up, testing the night air for the unique vibrations that hir spouse gave off, a pattern that was as familiar to Talis as hir own. Ze kept looking over hir shoulder, expecting to see slavers creeping up behind hir.

From the fifth alley ze checked, came the sound of soft moans and the unmistakable sense of Almoris. Talis rushed into the darkness, heedless of any danger. Almoris lay in shadows between two high buildings, in a spreading pool of blue blood. Ze moaned again and Talis fell to hir knees at hir spouse's side.

'What happened?' Talis asked, fear making hir voice sound harsh.

Almoris' eyelids fluttered and ze pushed hirself up onto hir elbows. 'More of them came up from the docks,' ze groaned. 'I didn't have a chance. Where's Juki?'

'Gone. We got separated and Vinhardt took hir. I heard everything but I couldn't stop it.' Talis ran hir hands over Almoris' body, looking for the source of the blood. At last ze found it; a shallow wound in hir side. They should be able to get back to the boarding house and treat it there. The rest of hir injuries appeared manageable; some bruising, the side of hir face was swollen and ze would be stiff and sore for days to come. 'Can you stand?'

'I think so.'

Almoris rolled onto hir side and then onto hands and knees. For a moment, ze rested there, hanging hir head and breathing heavily. Talis crouched at hir side and murmured reassurances. When Almoris was ready, Talis helped hir to stand and supported hir weight.

'Where is Batanel?' Almoris asked.

'I don't know,' Talis said, guiding hir spouse forward.

'We need to find hir.'

'We need to make sure the slavers have gone.'

'I can't believe they found us,' Almoris said, pausing and leaning against the wall for a moment.

'Someone must have betrayed us,' Talis said, voice tight. Hir antennae were scanning the area for any hint of Batanel. Nothing. All the stone of the buildings surrounding them could be blocking the signal though.

'Are you sure?' Almoris asked, squeezing hir eyes shut against the pain of hir wound.

'They came at us from both sides and you said more came up from the docks. That doesn't seem like a chance encounter to me.'

Almoris nodded slowly. 'Nyqam?'

'I hope so,' Talis muttered.

'What do you mean?'

Talis shook hir head. 'Never mind. Are you ready to go on?'

They made their way slowly to the end of the alley and peered around the corner. The street was deserted. Talis still supporting Almoris' weight, they walked towards the stairs that Batanel had climbed such a short time ago. The blue door above stood ajar, shadows filling the gap.

Talis looked doubtfully at the metal staircase and then back at hir spouse. 'Why don't you wait down here?'

'I'm not letting you go alone! What if there's someone up there, waiting for us?'

'Then I have a better chance of getting away if I don't have to worry about getting you back down the stairs safely,' Talis answered gently.

Almoris huffed out air in a sigh. 'I suppose you're right.'

Talis tucked Almoris into the space beneath the stairs,

shrouded in shadows. 'If I'm not back in five minutes, head for home and don't look back.'

Almoris huffed again but gave a sharp nod.

Talis crept to the bottom of the stairs and started up them, keeping to the edges of the treads. Still, it seemed as though ze made an inordinate amount of noise. Ze flinched a little with every creak and clang but no-one came to investigate. The door still stood ajar and all of hir senses were strained towards the gap, beyond which anything could be waiting. Batanel had gone into that room and not come back – at least not before Vinhardt had shown up. Was someone in there waiting for hir? Had ze been captured – or worse? Hir antennae stretched to the point of pain but still there was no sense of Batanel, or anyone else, close by.

Talis carried no weapon. If someone waited for hir on the other side of the door, then the only thing ze had on hir side was the element of surprise. Ze paused, crouching just beneath the top of the stairs. Ze took a couple of deep breaths then exploded into action, slamming the door open and throwing hirself through the opening, then rolling across the floor to the other side of the small room that ze found hirself in.

Ze fetched up against the wall and looked around. To hir left stood a bed, rumpled sheets hanging off the side along with a pair of maroon feet. The owner of the feet had not moved.

Talis stood up carefully. On the bed lay the body of someone ze could only assume to be Nyqam. The eyes were open and glazed, giving Talis a shiver of fear. There were no obvious wounds, but blood was smeared around the mouth and nose.

There was no-one else in the room.

Where is Batanel? Did ze do this?

Whatever had happened here, there was nothing that Talis could do to change it. Ze took a quick look around the room, anxious to return to Almoris but reluctant to leave without any more information. The room was small and dingy, the walls water-stained and dark with mould in the corners. At the bottom of the bed a travel bag lay open, clothes spilling out onto the floor. Talis quickly rifled through the bag, listening out for anyone approaching and feeling like a naughty child. The bag contained nothing useful. Dirty clothes, three decks of cards, a small token pouch and a notebook filled with observations about tides and weather patterns. Half a bottle of whisky stood on top of the chest of drawers against the opposite wall, with two smudged glasses. There was nothing here to shed any light on who had done this.

Talis walked to the door which now stood wide open and cautiously peered around the frame. The street below was still empty; a state that seemed suspicious to hir. But then, ze rarely came into this part of town. Perhaps people did not move around so much after dark further away from the factories. Ze stepped out and pulled the door closed behind hir.

At the bottom of the stairs, Almoris was waiting, a worried expression on hir face.

'Batanel?'

'Not here,' Talis answered. 'There was a body. Nyqam, I would guess.'

'You think Batanel did it?'

Talis wrung hir hands. 'I don't know. But we do know that Batanel went up there and didn't call for help or warn us that anything was amiss. Then we were ambushed by Vinhardt and now there's a dead person in the room. I don't think that we can make any assumptions about Batanel's loyalty at this stage.'

Almoris shook hir head. 'I don't know what to make of it.'

'We need to get you home. After your injuries have been treated will be time enough to figure this out.'

They took a roundabout route back to the boarding house, with Almoris taking frequent breaks. It was close to midnight when they pushed the back door open and stumbled into the kitchen. Talis helped Almoris into a chair at the table and leaned back against the wall for a moment. Hir back ached from stooping down to support hir spouse for so long and ze stretched, wincing at the twinges along hir spine.

A bucket beside the table held clear, fresh water from the well behind the boarding house. Talis muttered hir thanks to whoever had left the water here and ladled some into a bowl.

Ze placed the bowl on the table then held a hand above it, thinking of heat until the water began to steam. Ze helped Almoris to remove hir tunic and then dipped a cloth into the hot water before ever so gently beginning to clean the blood away from hir wound.

Almoris hissed and gripped the edge of the table in one pair of hands while lacing the fingers of the other pair so tightly that the colour left hir knuckles.

The wound was shallow, but the edges were ragged, and blood still seeped, tinged with tiny black threads. At first, Talis thought the threads were tiny pieces of fabric that had come from Almoris' clothing but ze had been wearing brown leggings with a beige tunic. As Talis stared at one of the threads on the cloth, trying to figure out what it was, it wriggled, edging back towards the wound.

Talis uttered a small squeal and threw the cloth down in revulsion.

'What is it?' Almoris asked, sounding alarmed.

'I don't know.' Talis took the cloth and showed it to Almoris. 'You see the little black thread?'

'Where?'

'Here,' Talis said, pointing to the …thing …with hir pinkie. 'It's moving, see?'

'I don't see anything.'

'How can you not see it? It's right there!' Talis fought against the panic that wanted to rise in hir like water shooting from a geyser.

'I'm sorry, Talis. I can't see any thread and certainly nothing that's moving.' Almoris looked closely at Talis, studying hir face. 'Are you sure there's something there?'

Talis closed hir eyes and counted to ten, trying not to snap. Ze opened hir eyes again and looked straight at the cloth.

There was no black thread.

'I could have sworn it was right there,' Talis said, picking the cloth up and peering at it. There was no sign at all of whatever ze thought ze had seen. 'I must have been seeing things.'

Talis went back to cleaning out the wound, checking it carefully. Ze saw no more of the black threads and no sign of anything unusual about the injury but ze could not shake the feeling that there was something deeply wrong.

The next morning, Talis got up at the usual time to prepare the morning meal and make sure the boarders did not think anything out of the ordinary had happened. Ze bantered with them and made sure to appear in good spirits, singing softly while ze worked, telling the boarders that Almoris had come down with a summer flu and would spend a few days in bed. That should be long enough for the worst of the injuries to fade.

When the house was finally empty, Talis heated some broth and took it up to the bedroom ze shared with Almoris. The shutters were still closed, leaving the room dark and vaguely claustrophobic. Almoris was a humped shape under several layers of blankets. The room smelled stale; Talis wrinkled hir nose. Ze set the cup of broth down on the small bookshelf next to the bed and pulled back the blankets. Almoris blinked at hir and ze stepped back, hands flying to hir mouth to supress a startled gasp.

Black threads wriggled across the surface of Almoris' eyes.

What are *they?* Talis forced hirself to step forward again and peered into hir spouse's eyes.

'What is it, Talis? What's going on?'

'There's … something … in your eye.' Talis went to the window and threw open the shutters, letting some light into the room.

Almoris rubbed hir eyes. 'Is it gone?'

Talis knelt beside the bed and studied Almoris. There was no sign of the black threads, just as there had been no sign of them last night after ze had looked away.

'Yes,' ze said, slowly, sitting back on hir heels. 'It seems to be.' *Am I seeing things that aren't there?*

Almoris propped hirself up on a pair of arms and rubbed hir face with the other hands. 'Oh, I ache all over.'

'Here,' Talis said, handing hir the cup of broth. 'There's some ralanger in there, it should soothe your pain.'

Almoris sat up and dangled hir feet over the side of the bed. Talis got up and began to move around the room, picking up clothing that had been discarded the night before.

'Any word from Batanel?' Almoris asked.

Talis shook hir head. 'Nothing. I don't want to write hir off but none of this looks good.'

Almoris sighed heavily and put hir head in hir heads. 'Do you really think Batanel could have betrayed us?'

'I don't know.' Talis perched on the side of the bed and took one of Almoris' hands in hir own. 'I don't want to think that. Batanel is my friend as much as yours. But Vinhardt had to get word of our plans from somewhere. Nyqam is dead and Batanel has disappeared. If ze didn't betray us, then who did?' Ze shrugged.

'What do we do now?'

'I should have thought of this last night, but did they see your face?' Talis asked, a sudden sense of urgency overcoming hir.

'No.' Almoris squeezed hir hand and then stood up, moving over to the window, which ze opened, letting in the cool morning air. 'At least, I don't think so. They attacked me from behind and once I was on the ground, I kept my arms up over my head.' Ze turned around, alarm on hir face. 'What about you? Vinhardt has seen you before – twice now! Ze could recognise you.'

'They were behind us and then on the other side of a wall. I still have no idea how they managed to get around there, to be in the exact place that Juki went over. I don't like it.'

'If Batanel had told them where to find us, ze couldn't have known which way you would run.'

'And if ze did betray us, it doesn't really matter whether they saw our faces or not – they know who we are and where we live.'

For a moment they both looked fearfully at the window. The normal morning sounds of the street drifted in through the open window.

'Perhaps it's time to move on,' Almoris said at last.

Talis looked away, letting hir gaze roam across the room, taking it all in. 'We worked so hard to build this life.'

'We always knew it might come to this, some day. That we might have to walk away and start over somewhere new.' Almoris walked over to Talis and reached up to cup hir face. 'At least we'll be together.'

Talis looked down at hir spouse. Almoris was everything

to hir. Hir soul. The air ze breathed. As long as they were together, ze could face anything. 'Alright,' ze said, leaning into Almoris' hand. 'But if we're going, let's go out with a bang.'

'What do you mean?'

'Let's get Juki back first.'

Five

Almoris waited until Talis left to get some supplies. They had decided that it was probably best not to be seen around the market they usually frequented – where all of this had started only a few days ago – so Talis would be making the trek across the colony to the other mid-level market, where no-one would know hir. This had the added advantage of making sure that ze would be away from the boarding house for the majority of the day.

Almoris tied hir long, curly hair into a braid and shrugged into a loose robe, wincing against the pull of the bandage around hir torso. Ze knew that Talis didn't want hir to leave the boarding house until ze had healed a little but time was a luxury they didn't have.

Ze hobbled down the stairs, telling hirself that the stiffness in hir muscles would wear off after ze had been moving for a while. In the kitchen, ze grabbed a bread roll off the cooling rack and filled a canteen with water then slipped out the back door into the courtyard at the rear of the boarding house. Almoris tipped hir face up, letting the morning sun warm hir skin and then pulled a flat cap on low and set off.

It didn't take long to realise that ze wasn't going to be able to walk the whole way to hir destination. The muscle soreness was increasing rather than wearing off and ze could feel exhaustion setting in already. Ze checked the tokens in hir pouch. Enough to get the hire-cart into the rich centre rings of Cortill and back again. Ze scurried along a zig-zagging path down the narrow streets until ze reached Red Brick Square.

Almoris went to the fountain in the middle of the square and scooped up some water, splashing it on hir face and muttering a quick prayer of thanks to the spirit of water that was said to inhabit this fountain. On the other side of the square, a small group stood together, studiously avoiding each other's gaze in the way of people who are forced to wait for something in public, surrounded by strangers, as if the very act of waiting was a form of idleness of which one should be ashamed.

The hire-cart was due any time now.

Almoris walked over and joined the waiting group just as the sounds of the hire-cart began to drift to their ears. The creak of the wheels, the driver's voice exhorting the cricks onwards and the high whine that the giant insects emitted when they were happy.

The cricks were visible first, two of them harnessed together, hopping into sight on their powerful legs, wings clipped to their sides. Next, the segmented cart swung into view, making jerky progress in its leather traces.

'Ho!' The driver pulled back on the reins and the cricks took one final hop, clicking their mandibles as they stopped in front of the waiting people.

The driver climbed down from hir seat with a groan and stretched, all four fists pressed into the small of hir back. Ze hooked a bag over the head of each of the cricks, fruit from the smell of it.

Almoris dug some tokens out of hir pouch and waited. A few passengers disembarked, and the driver spoke to them cheerily before turning to the group that were waiting. Almoris tried not to tap hir foot impatiently while the driver negotiated a price for the journey with each passenger.

'Where to?' The driver asked, approaching Almoris at last.

'The artisan ring, please.'

'Three tokens.' The driver turned hir head and spat to the side. 'Or five for the round trip. It would have to be my cart coming back, mind.'

'How often do you pass through there?' Almoris asked.

'Roughly every two hours. Can't be too exact with the cricks you know.'

'That's fine. I'll take the round trip, thanks. Two hours should be enough time for my business.'

The driver cocked hir head to the side, one antenna raising.

'It will soon be my spouse's hatchday,' Almoris said casually. 'I am looking for a gift for hir.'

'Ah,' the driver said, nodding and removing the bags from the cricks' heads. 'You're going to the right place then.'

Almoris sighed as ze took a seat on the busy cart, hir body

aching. Ze may have to visit the apothecary before hir return.

A bell jingled above the door when Almoris stepped into the shop. Dust motes danced in the sunlight and the sound of trickling water came from the other side of an arch covered by a delicately painted silk hanging.

Bronze sculptures stood on carefully lit pedestals, their warm glow adding to the welcoming feeling of the shop. Almoris wondered over to the wall, where some plaques hung, arranged in such a way that their designs complimented one another. Ze studied the lines and grooves worked into the buffed bronze, the flow and form clearly marking the work of a highly skilled craftsperson.

'Almoris, how nice to see you.'

Almoris turned around to see Xandire stepping into the room, the silk hanging falling back over the arch behind hir. Instead of the plain and sturdy leggings and tunic that Almoris and Talis favoured, Xandire wore wide-legged, silk trousers that shimmered as ze walked with a long blouse, tied at the waist with a belt that perfectly matched the aquamarine colour of hir skin.

Around hir eyes were the elaborate tattoos of the seed classes; the signal to one and all that these were the rulers of the colony and were not to be interfered with in any way. The punishment for anyone found to be wrongfully sporting such tattoos was death by burial in a tar pit.

'Xandire, I hope you're well?'

'In better health than you, from the look of it.' Xandire frowned at Almoris' battered appearance. 'What can I do for you?' Hir antennae stood tense above short, spiked, navy hair.

'It's something of a sensitive matter,' Almoris said, glancing at the door.

'Of course!' Xandire strode over to the door and twisted the lock. Ze took a sign from a small wooden unit beside a display table and hung it in the window.

It read: GONE FOR SUPPLIES, BACK IN AN HOUR.

'Shall we?' Xandire said, gesturing towards the archway with its silk hanging.

Almoris followed the artisan through to hir workroom. On

one table, sat large lumps of unworked bronze, waiting for Xandire to work hir magic. Another table held blank sheets, worked and polished to a beautiful gleam but not yet bearing any of the print work that Xandire was known for. At the rear of the room were two rocking chairs beside a small brazier which was currently unlit and a delicate stone fountain which provided clean water. On a small, intricately carved table between the two rocking chairs sat an oil lamp, burning with a warm, fragrant scent.

Almoris could never quite believe how different life was for the rich seed classes.

As a treasured offspring of the Prefect of Cortill, Xandire wanted for nothing. Ze would never have to live in fear of hir affinity being discovered; the very opposite was true. Ze was free to wield hir affinity openly. Hir skill with bronze was celebrated far and wide while those who were born to the poor outer reaches of Cortill hid their affinity, constantly in fear of the slave gangs who would press them into service in one of the factories for some imagined crime.

Everyone knew what went on and no one did anything about it. Well, almost no one.

'Tea?' Xandire asked, turning in a whirl of cloth.

'That would be most welcome.'

'Would you mind?' Xandire gestured towards the unlit brazier then lifted a kettle and filled it with water from the fountain.

Almoris pointed one hand towards the oil lamp and then flicked hir fingers towards the brazier. Flame leapt from one to the other and quickly took hold of the wood that sat ready. Almoris blew across hir fingers and the flame leapt, crackling happily.

'It's so much quicker when you do it,' Xandire said, smiling and hanging the kettle above the brazier. 'Now, what happened to you?'

Almoris explained about Juki and the ambush and by the time ze was finished, the tea had been brewed and they both sat sipping it in the rocking chairs.

'Do you truly think Batanel could have betrayed you?' Xandire asked, hir antennae quivering. 'Did ze know about me?'

'No. You know how close Talis likes to keep things. Mostly, the appeal of working with Batanel was that ze brought hir own contacts and opened new doors for us.'

Xandire sat back, one pair of hands cradling the teacup while the fingers of the other pair drummed on hir thighs. 'Was their anything special about this wood-wielder? What did you say hir name was?'

'Juki, and no. Not as far as I could tell anyway. Ze was young. Scared. Leaking all over the market when Vinhardt came across hir.'

'Then why now? Why hir?'

'I don't follow you,' Almoris said, inhaling the steam from the tea.

'Batanel has been working with you and Talis for months now and spent months before that gaining your trust, yes?'

'That's right.'

'So why betray you now. What does ze gain? And why did Vinhardt take only Juki? Surely ze must know about you and Talis now; both of you are powerful wielders, any of the factory owners would pay a fortune to have you in chains.'

Almoris frowned. 'I hadn't thought of that. We talked about how the slavers might know where we live now, but you're right, why not just take us last night?'

The two of them sat in silence, pondering this question, until a piece of wood popped in the brazier, sending sparks dancing into the air and startling them. The flecks of flame were drawn to Almoris and danced around hir head like a fiery crown. Ze flicked them away and they gradually drifted back to the brazier.

'I do think it's a good idea for the two of you to get away, for a while anyway. Perhaps tell your boarders there's been an emergency. Do you have relatives you could go to?'

Almoris shook hir head. 'We were both brought up by nest-guardians,' ze said. 'Talis was close with hirs, they keep in touch.'

'Well then, maybe you could tell people this nest-guardian is ill, and you are both going to take care of hir in hir final days. Then travel in the opposite direction.'

'That's not a bad idea,' Almoris said. 'We were thinking of heading for –,'

'Don't tell me,' Xandire said sharply. 'Just in case.'

Almoris paled. Xandire would never betray them of hir own accord.

'So, what help do you need from me?' Xandire asked, hir tone turning business-like. 'Tokens? A carriage? Travelling clothes?'

'We have provisions for all of that,' Almoris said. 'We always knew we might have to leave at short notice. It's … we want to try and rescue Juki before we go.'

'Are you out of your mind?' Xandire cried, exploding up and out of hir seat. 'How do you think to achieve that?'

'Well, first of all we need to find out where they're keeping hir.'

'And that's where I come in?' Xandire asked, pinching the bridge of hir nose. 'You think the Prefect will know.'

Almoris shrugged. 'We know that wielders aren't kept at the jail because it's an uncontrolled environment. But no matter how we've tried over the years, we've never been able to find out where Vinhardt takes them. So, we thought about who else would know where it is, and the only person we could come up with was the Prefect.'

'Just because ze is my parent doesn't mean I can waltz into hir house and start asking for information that I have no right to.' Xandire's antennae were trembling and hir voice was sharp with anger.

'I know that, Xandire, I'm not asking you to do anything that would put you at risk. Just listen, see if you hear any talk that would help. We'll do the rest.'

'This is more involved than I ever expected to be.' Xandire began pacing from one side of the workroom to the other. 'You know I'm happy to help out occasionally, arranging transport and the like, but you're asking me to go directly against my parent, who also happens to be the most powerful person in the colony. I agree with you that wielders shouldn't be made slaves just because of the status of their birth, but this, Almoris, this is too much.'

'Very well,' Almoris said, looking down at hir hands. 'While Juki was with us, ze told us about hir friend, Lessin, who had been a slave and had managed to escape during a fire. Juki didn't say too much about what conditions were like in the factory, but Lessin believed ze was about to be captured again and took hir own life rather than go back to slavery.'

Xandire turned away, putting hir face in hir hands.

'I know that you don't want other wielders to be treated this way. Juki is barely old enough to wield. Ze was terrified when we found hir, leaking all over the place. Ze made a wooden statue of Talis. It's some of the best work I've ever seen.'

Xandire shook hir head and perched on the edge of the rocking chair, sighing. 'Of course, I'll help. But I can't guarantee anything. And for the record, I think this is a really bad idea.'

'Thank you.' Almoris drained the last of hir tea and stood. 'I'd better go. I don't want to stay long enough to arouse suspicion.'

They made their way back through to the front room of the shop and Xandire unlocked the door, flipping over the sign.

'I'll be in touch over the next couple of days. I'll bring a plaque out to you or something. In the meantime, you should make preparations to run.'

'Thank you, my friend,' Almoris said, bowing hir head. Ze reached for the door but just as ze grasped the handle, Xandire stopped hir.

'I thought you said there was nothing special about Juki. So why do this? Why risk so much for hir.'

Almoris frowned. How could ze explain that it wasn't really about Juki? The young wielder had touched their hearts for sure but so had many of the others that they had helped over the years. In truth, this was about hirself and Talis, the legacy they would leave behind. If Juki was to be the last wielder they could help, then they had to make sure ze got away. They couldn't end their lives' work with a failure.

At last, Almoris said, 'If it's really over for us, then we're going to make sure we're never forgotten.'

Six

Xandire stepped out of the carriage just as the gong sounded announcing dinner. Ze had sent a runner to the Prefect, asking to move their weekly get-together forward to tonight, mentioning a workshop that ze wished to attend on their usual evening.

The Prefect stood in the doorway, subtly lit by coloured gas laps that hung on either side. Ze wore white tunic and trousers with a red sash, marking hir out as someone important. White was too impractical for anyone who had to do any sort of manual work.

Xandire looked up at hir parent and smiled, hir hearts fluttering inside hir thorax. Ze had been working with the underground for several years but ze had never done anything as direct as this.

'Good evening, Xandire,' the Prefect said, hir voice as gentle as the night breeze that danced through the blooms lining the path.

'Good evening, Prefect,' Xandire answered bowing hir head. 'Thank you for making time for me this evening.'

'You know you are always welcome here, treasured one.' The Prefect stepped inside the house, gesturing to indicate that Xandire should follow. 'It will be a simple meal this evening, just four courses.'

'I'm sure it will be delightful.'

The Prefect walked into a large room lined with bookshelves and headed straight for the drinks cabinet. Without asking, ze poured them both a drink of fermented goat's milk. Xandire carefully plastered a smile in place before hir parent turned around. Ze hated fermented goat's milk but the Prefect would insist that ze just needed to acquire the taste for it.

'So, why was it you wished to move our dinner up to tonight?' the Prefect said.

'Werick is holding a workshop on displaying art for maximum appeal. I thought it sounded interesting, and useful for the shop.'

'Is business slow?' the Prefect asked, sounding concerned.

'Not at all,' Xandire smiled. 'My pieces are selling well and I'm definitely becoming better known. Why, only yesterday I had a request from a Cordish merchant to take five of the smaller plaques.' Ze sipped the goat's milk and supressed a grimace. 'I just wish to be the best I possibly can be. I want to bring honour to your name.'

'You do that already,' the Prefect said, smiling. 'Is there anything I can do to help you achieve your ambitions?'

'No,' Xandire said, following hir parent to the dining room, where the table was beautifully set, and the Prefect's newest spouse was already seated and waiting for them. 'It's all about improving my own skills at the moment.'

'Well, let me know if anything changes.'

'Of course,' Xandire said, taking a seat and nodding to the new spouse before turning back to hir parent. 'How was your day? Have your plans for a new factory near the docks been progressing?'

'Slowly, slowly, but I'm sure to find the right business partner for it soon. None of the current factory owners want to expand. Honestly, they're all so short-sighted; moaning all the time about the cost of supplies, about being forced to close down for six hours a day, about how much workers cost and how little they do.'

Xandire carefully kept hir gaze on the bowl of crab soup in front of hir. Ze had grown up listening to hir parent talking about the factory owners and other influential people in the seed classes. They were nothing but a group of greedy larvae, treating their workers poorly and forcing wielders into slavery just so that they could profit from the affinities without paying for them. They were so short-sighted, not able to see that if they paid their workers appropriately, there would be more people who could afford to buy the finished products. Idiots.

'It must be very frustrating for you,' Xandire said neutrally.

'Well, yes, but it all goes with the position that has been so graciously bestowed upon me,' the Prefect said smoothly.

'I don't know how you manage it all.' Xandire leaned back in hir chair as a servant came in to the clear the table for the next course. 'Having to keep the factory owners in line, deal with merchant disputes, arrange trade agreements … and on top of all that you have to hear trials! I wish I had your capacity for juggling work.'

The new spouse fiddled with hir cutlery. Ze had not yet said a word. Xandire hadn't even bothered to learn this one's name. Ze was the latest of twenty and would not be likely to last much longer than the others from what Xandire had seen of hir. Ze crept around like a sand-crawler, forever hiding. The Prefect grew bored with spouses quickly; Xandire was amazed that this one had kept hir attention for long enough to be bonded.

'You flatter me, treasured one,' the Prefect said, hir smug smile belying hir words. 'I'm sure you could manage everything that I do if you decided to turn your hand to it.'

'Not at all,' Xandire said, laughing. 'I am an artist and I excel in one area. You are skilled in many areas. Take the trials for instance, I wouldn't know the first thing about how they work.'

'It is not so difficult,' hir parent answered expansively. 'I simply listen to the facts of the case and apply the law.'

The next course arrived and Xandire nibbled at the sweetened pastry that had been placed in front of hir, taking the opportunity to plan the next thing ze would say. Ze hoped to flatter the Prefect into telling hir about the young woodwielder, but it must be handled delicately.

'But the law gives you some discretion, does it not?' Xandire asked.

'It does, yes, but less than you might think.'

'How do you know if the person brought before you is actually guilty of a crime?'

'I don't understand,' the Prefect said, looking baffled.

'Well, you have to determine guilt, don't you? Or am I misunderstanding?' Xandire gave a self-deprecating laugh. 'I told you I wasn't cut out for this sort of thing.'

'Ah, I see. Yes, I do determine guilt, officially, but I trust the peacekeepers in our colony. If they are confident that the person they bring before me has broken our laws, then I'm going to take them at their word.'

'Of course, I hadn't thought of that,' Xandire said with

a tone of admiration. *Oh, you clever parasite. If the tide ever turns and you have to justify enslaving so many wielders, you can just claim you were misled by the peacekeepers, that all you were guilty of is being too trusting.* 'This baitan is delicious,' ze said, licking crumbs of flaky pastry from hir lips.

'Reyam is a wonderful baker,' the Prefect said, smiling at the new spouse.

'I must ask you to teach me how to make this,' Xandire said. 'Baking is another skill that I do not have.'

Reyam gave a half-smile. 'Of course, Artisan, it would be an honour.'

The conversation wondered onto safer topics while Xandire contemplated how to lead hir parent to discuss the wood-wielder without giving away the fact that ze knew anything ze shouldn't. Since the case wouldn't have been heard yet, it wouldn't be public knowledge. After the third course had been served, ze tried a different tactic.

'I heard there was a disturbance at the docks last night,' Xandire said casually, spooning creamed vegetables onto hir plate.

'What sort of disturbance?' the Prefect asked sharply.

'Some Akrian sailor found dead apparently.' Xandire took a long drink of water before continuing, studiously avoiding hir parent's gaze. 'It was all the talk in the artisan circle today. There was one rumour that ze owed a large gambling debt to one of our wealthier merchants and tried to set sail without paying. But I also heard that ze took the wrong lover and was robbed and another version was that ze had enemies back home who decided to rid themselves of hir where they would be less likely to fall under such suspicion.'

The Prefect visibly relaxed. 'You shouldn't listen to such nonsense.'

'It's hard not to. This sort of thing doesn't happen much. Or at least not that I'm exposed to. It's fun to try and work out what happened to hir, although I suppose it's callous to say so.'

The Prefect smiled indulgently. 'And what do you think happened?'

Xandire put down hir cutlery and allowed hir hands to wave around, excited. 'Well, my favourite theory was that ze has a lover here but it's someone of high class, someone that couldn't possibly bond with a sailor. So, the sailor had to get money from somewhere, right? So ze started gambling – but the cards didn't go hir way and now ze was in an even worse position. So then, ze stole something valuable in Akros and fled back here to sell it and claim hir lover.'

'So, any number of people could be suspects,' Reyam said softly. Xandire had almost forgotten the spouse was there.

The Prefect chuckled. 'It's nothing so dramatic, I'm afraid.'

Xandire allowed hir hands to fall into hir lap, trying to project disappointment. 'Of course, you know about it already, don't you? Was it gambling debts?'

'A robbery gone wrong, we think. A runaway was caught, a wielder of all things.'

Xandire's hearts sped up, pounding a complicated rhythm. 'Well that's disappointingly mundane. Sounds like the robber is more interesting than the victim.'

The Prefect laughed. 'Don't be too heartbroken, treasured one. It is almost time for dessert.'

'My favourite part of any meal,' Xandire said, smiling and pushing hir plate away. 'What will happen to the wielder?'

'Slavery,' the Prefect said, shrugging. 'For how long will depend on the circumstances and whether ze will co-operate.'

'What happens to a wielder waiting for sentencing?' Xandire asked, frowning, as if the idea had only just occurred to hir. 'Is there a special wing of the jail or something?'

'Usually I try deal with them on the day they are caught. In more complicated cases, like this one, there's a warehouse that has been adapted to accommodate wielders. Far too dangerous to keep them with the normal folks.'

'Not near here, I hope!' Xandire exclaimed, giving an exaggerated shudder and trying not to grind hir teeth at that 'normal' comment.

'Of course not,' the Prefect said solicitously. Ze reached across the table and patted Xandire's hand. 'It's out the east side of the colony, near the foundries and iron-works.'

'That's a relief,' Xandire said, sitting back as dessert was brought in.

Seven

It was the morning of the third day since Juki had been taken and Talis was frustrated beyond measure. So far, ze had been able to find no hint of where Vinhardt might have taken the young wood-wielder. Every surface in the boarding house was gleaming; Talis cleaned to work out hir frustration. Now ze was restless, pacing around the building like a caged beast. Two of their boarders were upstairs; ze hoped that they just assumed ze and Almoris had been arguing.

Ze hadn't seen any more of the black threads on (*in?*) Almoris since the morning after the ambush. Ze was starting to think it really had been some sort of hallucination, perhaps brought on by the stress of losing Juki and then seeing Almoris injured again so soon after the robbery. Still, something about that didn't sit right with hir. Talis was not a person prone to flights of fancy. Ze was practical. Steadfast. A lot of hir sense of self was tied up in that.

Ze prowled around the lower floor of the boarding house, cloth in hand, scrubbing at already-spotless woodwork. There had been no word from Batanel, reinforcing the idea that ze had been the one to betray them. Something didn't feel right about it though. Talis growled in frustration. Perhaps ze was just being sentimental, not wanting to accept the truth.

Ze stalked into the front room and hir gaze immediately came to rest on the small wooden statue that Juki had given hir. Tears prickled the backs of hir eyes and ze turned away. They had let Juki down. If Almoris had never gone out looking for hir, it's possible that ze would still be free. For Talis, that was at the root of hir driving need to get the young wood-wielder back.

Talis rubbed hir antennae and slowly brought hir emotions back under control. A moment later, there was a knock at the door. Talis scrubbed at hir face as ze walked to the door and opened it, half-expecting to see Vinhardt. It was a young person with very pale blue skin, wearing a grey uniform and flat cap.

'Can I help you?' Talis asked.

'I have the plaque you ordered from Xandire,' the young person said, holding out a package.

Talis frowned. They hadn't ordered any plaque that ze knew about. 'Thank you,' ze said, accepting the parcel and closing the door. *So, that's why Almoris looked so exhausted the other night. Ze went to see Xandire while I was out.*

Ze made hir way upstairs, muttering to hirself about hir spouse's stubbornness.

'You have a package,' Talis said, entering the bedroom and tossing the package onto the bed beside Almoris, who was sitting up, reading a book on foraging. Talis reckoned if it came to point that they were relying on a book to find safe food, they would both probably die. Ze had to admire Almoris' optimism though.

Almoris tore open the package and took out a note, which ze read aloud.

'Dear Almoris, please forgive the unplanned delivery but ever since yesterday morning I have been feeling as though I'm being watched. I'm probably overreacting but I decided it was best to be safe, for all our sakes. What you seek can be found on the outskirts of the colony, in a warehouse in the metal working district. I wish you both the best of luck and hope to see you again soon. Please, wherever the world leads you, take the enclosed plaque with my love. Xandire.'

'What do you seek?' Talis asked. 'Is it Juki? Did Xandire find out where Juki is somehow?'

Almoris nodded. 'I went to see Xandire the day after the ambush to see if ze could get any information from the Prefect. I wasn't sure ze would be able to, but I had to try.'

'It seems that you made the right decision. I do wish you had discussed it with me first though. We may have put Xandire at risk. If we are being watched …'

'I know,' Almoris said, bowing hir head. 'But it was the best chance I could think of. Xandire will be alright. There's no way ze'll be enslaved; the Prefect will protect hir.'

'There are many warehouses in the metal-working district. How will we find the right place?'

'Head out there in time for the shift-change and note the ones that no-one comes out of, then investigate them?'

Talis twisted the cloth that ze still held. 'We should be ready to leave straight from there. Just in case.'

'We'll have to travel light, my love.'

'I know.' Talis looked wistfully around the bedroom they had shared for the last nine years. 'I'll miss this place.'

'As will I. We've been happy here, haven't we?'

'Yes.' Talis walked over to Almoris and kissed hir. 'But I'll be happy wherever we go as long as I'm with you.'

They set off late in the afternoon, in a small carriage that Almoris had purchased the day before. They had been saving tokens for years, knowing that sooner or later this day would come. They had packed only a few changes of clothes, some food, the plaque from Xandire and the statue that Juki made. They both sat on the driver's bench, not speaking as the crick pulled them away from their home.

They had spoken to the boarders who were in the house and explained that they had received news that Talis' nest-guardian was very ill and wasn't expected to make it. The boarders were sympathetic; Talis often spoke of hir youth with fondness.

As far as the boarders were concerned, Talis and Almoris were going to visit and stay until it was over. Almoris had arranged for someone to come in take care of the cooking and cleaning for the time being. If all went well, they would ask Xandire to arrange the sale of the boarding house after they were settled somewhere new.

If things didn't go well, the boarders would be on their own.

Their carriage rattled and bounced along the cobbled roads of the mid-colony, heading towards the geriatric zone. As they crossed the bridge out of their own neighbourhood, Talis closed hir eyes and tried to plan ahead. They were being foolhardy. Ze knew that. They had no idea where they were going, no knowledge of the layout of the warehouse in question, no idea if Juki would still be there and no previous experience at this type of thing.

It didn't matter. Neither of them could let this go.

They had to assume that if ze was still there, Juki would be guarded by at least one slaver. Neither Talis nor Almoris had any experience with violence; the underground worked by staying in the shadows, remaining unseen and unsuspected. Still, they were not unprepared. Talis let hir hand fall onto the small axe that hung from hir belt, questioning whether ze could actually bring hirself to use it to harm someone, if it came to that. Then ze heard the sound of Vinhardt striking Juki on the other side of that wall and ze knew the answer.

The movement of the carriage lulled hir into a half-doze and ze dreamed of the day of the ambush. Hir mind took hir back over every detail, seeking some clue that all of this was going to happen.

Ze remembered Juki giving hir the statue, how touched ze had been. How Juki had asked hir to go with them. The young wielder had been so frightened and ze had turned to Talis to feel safe. And Talis had let hir down.

Talis' eyes flew open and ze sat bolt upright. 'It was a last-minute change,' ze said, gripping Almoris' arm.

'What was?'

'We were never meant to go with Batanel and Juki that night. Batanel was meant to go on hir own, we only went because Juki asked me to.'

Almoris glanced at hir. 'Ye-es.'

'I can't believe I didn't think of it earlier.'

'But, what difference does it make?'

'Surely, if Batanel had planned the ambush, ze wouldn't have wanted us to come along.'

'If I recall correctly, ze wasn't too happy about it.'

'Oh, ze was a little grumpy but ze made no effort to discourage us from coming. Why risk everything that way, if ze had made the arrangements to hand Juki over?'

A few moments passed in silence as they both thought through the implications. They were passing through the geriatric zone now, the shabby but serviceable district to which drones who were too old to work were relegated. The buildings were small and low-to-the-ground, with wide doors and level entrances. Most were fading, crumbling on places, but clean and tidy. The streets were quiet; very few people moved around the zone. Talis wondered how they occupied themselves when no longer in work.

'Only five people knew anything was happening that night,' Almoris said, keeping hir eyes on the road while ze spoke. 'You, me, Batanel, Juki and Nyqam. We know that neither of us told anyone and Juki didn't know where we were going, so ze *couldn't* have told anyone. Quite apart from the fact that ze spent the days before the ambush hiding in our attic room. Ze didn't have the opportunity to tell anyone.'

'So, Batanel or Nyqam.'

'If Nyqam was working with Vinhardt then why would the slavers kill hir?'

'Unless Batanel killed hir, when ze realised we had been ambushed.'

'That's possible … but it doesn't feel right. If Batanel had no part in the ambush and was in a position to kill Nyqam, why not come and help us? Why not get in touch since then?'

Talis sighed. 'It doesn't make sense.'

'It still seems most likely that Batanel intended to sell Juki to Vinhardt. The fact that ze has disappeared supports that, as much as it pains me to say so.'

Talis looked for flaws in Almoris' reasoning but couldn't find any. 'You're probably right,' ze said with a sigh.

The bitter taste of disappointment flooded hir mouth. For a moment, ze had thought that perhaps their friend had been innocent after all, that ze had rushed to judgement. Hir heart had lifted and ze had realised for the first time just how much this had been weighing on hir for the last few days. But what Almoris had said made sense and once more it seemed that Batanel was not the person they had thought.

The buildings around them were gradually growing darker, soot staining the stone deeper as they moved into the metal working district. Here, the fires were kept hot all day long, so that the surrounding area began to look as dark as the factories themselves. Not to mention the workers. One could usually spot a metalworker in the street from the almost-permanent stains on their hands and most of the way up their forearms.

The foot traffic in the street was steadily increasing as workers made their way towards the factories for the shift change. Almoris drew the carriage to a halt and leaned towards Talis, nuzzling hir cheek.

'You take the north side of the main street and I'll take the south,' Almoris said. 'We'll meet on the main street at the end of the shift change and compare notes.'

'I remember,' Talis said with a wry smile.

'I love you.'

'I love you too. Be careful.' With that, Talis turned and hurried away.

Before leaving the boarding house, Talis and Almoris had rubbed ash onto their clothing and skin in an effort to blend in better with the metalworkers but Talis saw now that it really hadn't been enough. Although hir hands were darkened, they did not have the look of ground-in soot – it was clear that Talis could wash hir stains off. Hir relative cleanliness would make hir stand out. Glancing around, ze tucked hir hands under the light traveling cloak that ze wore and pulled it tighter around hirself.

Talis quickened hir pace, determined to see every factory and warehouse on the north side before the end of the shift change. Fortunately, shift change usually took the best part of an hour. First, the workers arriving for the next shift would queue outside, waiting for the whistle to blow and the supervisors to open the doors and let them in, one-by-one, marking their presence on that day's report. Only after the workers entering the building had arrived at their station, were the previous shift released. They were allowed to exit the building after being searched to make sure that no-one was trying to steal tools or parts.

That was for the paid workers - as far as Talis was aware, the slaves - those there under punishment of law - were never allowed to leave the building. They slept in crowded dorms inside the factories and were escorted between them and their workstations by guards who were not slow to use physical punishment.

Talis maintained hir pace as people around hir peeled off, passing through gates in the high wrought-iron fences that ringed each factory. Ze scanned each building, looking for signs of occupation – light coming from inside, windows open – but no queue of workers waiting to be logged in.

None on the main street.

Ze turned left, along the side of the last building in the row and then took another left, onto the street that ran parallel to the one ze had just come down. In this way, Talis worked hir way past all of the factory and warehouse buildings on the north side of the main street. Ze saw only two likely locations for where Juki was being kept. By the time ze met with Almoris, back on the main street, ze was tired and disheartened. Ze climbed up onto the driver's bench and rested hir head in hir hands.

'Did you find anything?' Almoris asked.

'Two possibilities,' Talis answered with a sigh. 'You?'

'Just one, and I don't think it's very likely. It looked abandoned. There were smashed windows and signs of water damage at some point.'

'Why did you think there might be someone using it?' Talis asked, frowning.

'The drag marks on the ground behind the gates look fresh. As though people have still been going in and out.'

'Alright. So, three buildings to look at more closely.'

'We're in a better position that I thought we would be,' Almoris said. 'Business must be good in this part of the colony.'

'I suppose it always will be for metal workers,' Talis mused.

'Take us to your first building,' Almoris said, handing over the reins.

They tied the crick to a fence behind the first building and then walked through the open gate. They carried a parcel wrapped in cloth, which they would claim to be delivering to Foreman Gantz, if they were challenged. There was no-one around, however, and no need for their ruse. It looked as though there hadn't been anyone around for a long time, though Talis was sure that ze had seen a light inside when ze had passed earlier. At the rear of the building they found a small, wooden door, propped open. A quick peek inside showed the detritus of people living here the remains of cooking fires and some piles of clothing and blankets. Nothing suggested that Vinhardt or hir gang had ever been here.

They fared no better at the second building, a small warehouse that appeared to be in use. People were milling around outside when Talis and Almoris drove passed in the carriage. Boxes were being loaded into a cart, quickly and efficiently. This must be a warehouse belonging to a foreign merchant – all the Slyvoan factory owners followed the same shift pattern, as decreed by the Prefect.

'Soot and ashes,' Talis cursed. 'We're never going to find Juki.'

'Let's go and take a look at the building on the south side. Maybe we'll be lucky.'

Talis didn't answer, just passed over the reins and hunched forward, head bowed.

Dusk had fallen by the time they pulled the carriage to a halt outside the final building. There was a clear air of abandonment here – there were no signs outside, the main doors were rusted and at one end of the building, the walls sagged, water marks reaching higher than Talis's head.

The only windows were around the upper story of the building and a few were broken, covered with planks of wood, nailed on half-heartedly. A metal staircase led up to a door and a catwalk around the building.

The gates were ajar and cautiously, they stepped through. The ground squelched beneath their feet and Talis looked down, frowning. Ze focussed on the water, seeking the source.

'Almoris, I don't think this is it,' ze said after a moment. 'There's an underground river running right through here. That must be the cause of the water damage. That whole building is likely to be unsafe.'

'Is there any danger from the river now?'

Talis paused, concentrating again. 'No,' ze answered at last. 'The water is sluggish just now, running low in its channel.'

'Alright. Well, we probably won't find anything but let's take a look anyway, since we're here.'

Hand in hand, they crept towards the building, the soggy ground sucking at their feet and slowing their pace, until they reached the paved area in front of the building. Almoris was limping slightly, though trying to hide it and Talis insisted that they take a moment to rest. While Almoris tried to stretch out some of the tiredness from hir still-healing body, Talis leaned against the rusted door.

Frowning, ze turned around and placed all four hands against the metal.

'This is odd,' ze said in a low voice, beckoning Almoris over. 'The rust doesn't go all the way though. I think this is just a thin sheet of rusted metal placed on top of the real door. The moisture stops far too close to the surface for this to be real.'

'I can't think of any innocent reason for someone to do that,' Almoris said, studying the door. 'Are you sure, though? There has obviously been flooding here at some point.'

Talis thought for a moment. 'I can't be certain. The rust definitely doesn't go all the way through, but I can't be sure why.' Suddenly, hir antennae stretched out towards the wall, quivering. 'I can feel something.'

'What is it?'

'There's a familiar vibration in there. It might be Juki, but I can't be sure. All this water around us is distracting me, drowning out whoever is inside.'

With a glance at each other, they set off towards the stair-case that led up to the windows. Talis removed hir shoes and tied the laces together, hanging hir footwear around hir neck and Almoris followed suit. If there was someone inside the building, they didn't want to alert them to presence of intruders.

Talis crept up the stairs first, hir mind pulled back to the night of the ambush, when ze had climbed similar stairs outside of Nyqam's room. At least ze could see that no threat was waiting at the top this time. Still, the parallels made the hair on the back of hir neck stand on end. Ze almost screamed when Almoris brushed a hand over hir back.

Almoris leaned in close, putting hir lips close to Talis's ear. 'Look,' ze breathed pointing to one of the partially boarded up windows.

From this angle, they could see the warm glow cast by an oil lamp, flickering in the gloom. Talis drew in a sharp breath. *There's someone inside!* Hir hearts started beating faster and ze forced hirself to breathe deeply and slowly. Hir hands were trembling so ze clasped them in front of hir. *It's normal to be afraid but Juki needs you. You can do this.*

Ever so slowly and carefully, they climbed the last few stairs and crept towards the window. Almoris kept watch along the catwalk while Talis peered between the haphazardly placed boards into the room below.

The inside of the warehouse looked smaller than the outside. Talis glanced from one end of the building to the other. *Are there rooms all around the outside walls?* Still pondering that question, Talis shifted position to get a better view and let out an audible gasp, despite hir determination to be quiet.

At the far left of the building, from Talis's viewpoint, were three glass boxes. Tall enough for all but the tallest person to stand in, they looked to be only about three feet deep and the same width. They must have been designed to hold wielders; for some reason that nobody understood, affinity magic could not pass through glass. Around the room, oil lamps stood on stands of wood, their glow dancing across the glass. Against the wall opposite where Talis stood there were crates stacked, one on top of the other.

Talis moved again, peering to the right of the building. In the glow of lamplight, four people sat around a small table, playing cards. From this angle, none of them looked familiar. Talis was quite sure that Vinhardt wasn't here, but ze could not have identified any of the people below. Ze stepped back and gestured for Almoris to come to the window. Hir smaller spouse could not see through the gap so Talis bent and offered hir hands for Almoris to step into.

A moment later and a strangled moan told hir that Almoris had just seen the glass cells. Talis shivered at the thought of being held like that. The old, familiar anger burst into flame in hir stomach. *How dare they! Even cricks are treated better than that!*

All of a sudden, Almoris had dropped down to hir side, lips close to hir ear again. 'Let's get away from the building so we can talk.'

Talis nodded and together they descended the stairs even more carefully than they had climbed them.

This must be the place that Xandire told us about, but there was no sign of Juki, Talis thought. *Are we too late? Has ze been assigned to a factory already?*

When they reached the bottom of the stairs, Almoris pointed back towards the gate and Talis nodded. They had to decide what to do now. Should they wait and see if Juki showed up? Or give up on their plan to rescue hir and get out of Cortill before Vinhardt came looking for them?

'Well, Derryl, looks like I owe you two tokens. They did show up tonight.'

Talis and Almoris whirled as one. Emerging from the shadows beneath the metal staircase were two large people, both armed with crossbows and grinning.

'I think you must have us confused with someone,' Almoris said, spreading hir hands to show they were empty. 'We were just looking for somewhere to spend some time alone.'

'Oh yes?' The slaver on the right said, laughing. 'And why would that be.'

'Well, we're not supposed to be together,' Almoris said, hesitating. 'We're, um, bonded to other people.'

'Isn't that a coincidence, Derryl?' the same slaver said. 'Here we are, expecting a visit from one pair and a totally different pair just stumble our way.'

'You look like you had an unpleasant experience, friend,' Derryl said, staring hard at Almoris. 'Down by the docks perhaps?'

'Fell off a ladder a few days ago,' Almoris said, the muscles in hir jaw undermining hir casual tone of voice.

'I'm sure you won't mind coming inside to wait for our boss to arrive. We'll get this cleared right up.'

'Actually, we really should leave,' Talis said, taking a step backwards.

The slaver who had done most of the talking dropped the pretence and pointed hir weapon straight at Almoris. 'Inside. Now.'

Talis and Almoris exchanged a pained glance. They had no choice but to comply. For now.

Eight

The scent of damp and mould assaulted their nostrils as soon as they were forced inside the building. Beneath that there were other smells; smells that spoke of violence and horror. Talis's antennae quivered and ze fought the urge to flee or to fight, whatever the cost. Ze reached for the calmer, more calculating part of hirself to drown out the baser instincts. Their captors had followed them in and closed the door with a heavy bang behind them. Talis gave a start and Almoris squeezed hir hand.

The three cells that Talis had seen from the window seemed to have a weight that pulled at hir attention. As much as ze tried to force hir gaze away from them, ze kept finding hirself staring at them again, imaging the sheets of glass separating hir from Almoris. Ze stepped to the side, closer to hir spouse.

On the wall behind the table, where the four people playing cards had turned to watch proceedings, were three more cells, directly beneath the window that Talis had peered through. Juki huddled in one of them, hir arms wrapped around hir legs, knees to hir chest, head hidden.

'Juki!' Talis cried out, ending any chance they had to pretend they were here by chance.

The young wood-wielder looked up, resigned rather than startled. Hir face was swollen and bruised on one side where ze must have been struck, more than once. Hir eyes brimmed with tears and ze lifted one pair of hands to cover hir face.

Talis ran towards the cage, only to have one of their captors grab hir by the hair and haul hir back. Fire flowed over hir scalp just before ze was pulled off hir feet. Ze fell onto hir behind and caught hir tongue between hir teeth. Blood filled hir mouth and ze turned hir head and spat. *You'll pay for that.*

Almoris had turned to help, only to find a large knife at hir side, the tip pressing into hir skin just above the section of shell that protected hir organs. Ze froze, having to look on helplessly as Talis carefully got to hir knees and then stood, glowering at the person who had grabbed hir hair.

'Stay away from the cell.' Vinhardt stepped out from a door at the back of the large room. 'You've interfered with my pet's training quite enough already.'

'What are you talking about?' Talis demanded, looking from Vinhardt to Juki. Ze had a sinking feeling in hir gut.

Vinhardt didn't answer, instead gesturing to the people behind them. 'Please escort our guests to their own accommodation.' Ze turned to the four at the table. 'Your services will no longer be required. We can manage these two.'

The people around the table got up swiftly, tossing their cards down and hurrying towards the door that led outside.

Decoys, to make it look as though everyone was inside. But now ze doesn't want witnesses. Talis felt panic begin to gnaw at hir insides. Vinhardt no doubt planned to torture them in the hope of gaining information about the underground.

Talis and Almoris were roughly grabbed and shoved across the floor towards the cells they had seen from above. Talis wanted to fight, to do anything to stop them putting hir in that glass box, but one of their captors still held a knife close to Almoris and the fear that hir spouse would be hurt was all the inducement required to make Talis behave. Ze was docile as ze was shoved inside the cell, more upset at not being able to reach Almoris than at the glass pressing in all around hir. Almoris was forced into the cell beside hir, close enough to touch if it wasn't for the sheets of glass that separated them.

Juki was sobbing, hir cries muffled. Talis wished ze could go to the young wielder and comfort hir. Or shake hir.

'I'm sorry,' Juki wailed. 'I'm so sorry.'

'Shut up,' Vinhardt said in a bored tone. 'You are honestly one of the most pathetic creatures I've ever come across.'

'Was it you, Juki? Did you betray us?' Talis asked, forcing the words past the tightness in hir chest.

Vinhardt strode with surprising speed to the side of Juki's cage and slammed hir hand against the glass wall of the cell. Juki flinched back, cringing like a rat in sudden light.

'You will not speak, slave,' Vinhardt growled. 'You have forgotten your place.'

The door crashed open with enough force to make the walls shake and Talis jumped so much that ze banged hir head on the roof of hir cell. A hooded figure stormed into the centre of the room, dragging someone on a rope behind hir. The captive was also hooded but the quality of their clothing was very fine. Not at all the usual rags that the poor wielders who ended up as slaves wore.

Talis glanced fearfully at Almoris and saw that hir spouse had gone pale, hir gaze fixed on the person who had been dragged in on a rope.

'Almoris,' Talis said in as low a voice as ze could manage. 'Are you alright? Are you hurt?'

'It's Xandire,' Almoris answered, not looking away from the figure on the floor.

Talis looked back, hir breath catching in hir chest. *Could it be?*

The figure at the front yanked on the rope on the person at the other end was knocked to hir knees, a harsh cry forced from hir.

'Here is another wielder for your auctions, Vinhardt.' The voice of the Prefect was unmistakable. 'Take this faithless off-spring and do as you wish with it.'

'It is you who are faithless,' Xandire spat, pushing hir-self to hir feet and throwing back the hood that covered hir face, despite the rope around all four wrists. 'You abuse your position to use the skills of others for your own gain. I am ashamed to be your kin!'

The Prefect spun and hit Xandire in the face with a vicious back-handed blow that knocked the bronze-wielder to the floor once more.

Talis held onto the bars in front of hir, looking on help-lessly, frustration boiling in hir gut.

'These are the others?' The Prefect waved a hand in the direction of Talis and Almoris.

'Yes, your grace,' Vinhardt answered obsequiously. 'They arrived tonight looking for the wood-wielder, just as you predicted.'

'You two are bonded, are you not?' the Prefect said, look-ing between Almoris and Talis.

Neither of them answered. Talis stared at the Prefect with a defiant tilt to hir chin, hir antennae quivering with an unset-tling mixture of fear and rage.

'You will answer me,' the Prefect said, voice low and

menacing.

Talis glared but did not speak.

'Very well.' The Prefect tugged on Xandire's rope, knocking the bronze-wielder off balance, just as ze was trying to regain hir feet. In two quick movements, the Prefect had stepped behind hir offspring and wrapped the rope around hir neck. Ze dragged Xandire round to face the cells that Talis and Almoris were in and began to tighten the rope. Xandire made gagging sounds and clawed at the rope, struggling for air. Xir feet scrabbled at the floor and hir face darkened to an alarming shade.

Talis slammed hir hands repeatedly against the glass, until hir skin was hot and stinging but ze the glass did not so much as move. Ze kicked at it but could not draw hir leg back enough to get the force required to break the thick glass.

'Yes!' Almoris cried out, reaching through the bars. 'Yes, we're bonded. Leave Xandire alone.'

The Prefect allowed the rope to go slack and Xandire slumped to the floor, gasping for breath.

Talis felt sick. How could ze have allowed that awful person to hurt their friend without acting to stop it? Why had it been up to Almoris to break their silence? Ze had always thought hirself brave, strong. Had ze been wrong?

'Make sure they are sent to separate factories,' the Prefect said to Vinhardt.

'No!' Almoris shouted. 'Please, do not separate us. Please.'

Talis found that ze still could not speak. If ze could have, ze would have told Almoris not to protest – it would only make things worse. *How could we have been so foolish? To think we could just walk in here and rescue Juki. To think we were capable of dealing with these people. They've known our every move. I can't believe how naïve we have been.*

'And the other two, your grace? Do you have any special instructions for them?' Vinhardt clasped both pairs of hands, and lowered hir head in a subservient posture.

The Prefect stared at Xandire for a long moment before answering. 'No. Do with them as you see fit.'

Xandire stared hatred into hir parent from the floor and Talis wanted to weep. All of this was hir fault. Ze had been so determined to get Juki back. If only they had run the night of the ambush. Ze and Almoris might have gotten away and Xandire would have remained undiscovered.

The Prefect wandered over to stand in front of Almoris' cell and opened a sliding panel high in the side wall.

'I believe you have something that belongs to me,' ze said, taking a ball of black, shimmering material unlike anything Talis had ever seen before, from a pocket in hir cloak.

Ze waved a hand over the ball, muttering and cooing in a voice too low for Talis to make out the words. Almoris had shrunk back, pressing against the back wall of the cell.

'What are you doing?' Talis asked, voice hoarse with fear. 'Leave hir alone!'

Almoris began to tremble, hir whole body shaking like ze was freezing. Hir eyes took on a glazed cast that struck an ice-cold blade of fear into Talis's hearts. A grunting, groaning noise came from Almoris just before ze started foaming at the mouth.

'Stop it!' Talis screamed. 'Please, stop hurting hir!'

Xandire pushed hirself unsteadily to hir feet and moved towards the Prefect, arms outstretched, but ze was grabbed by Derryl, who forced Xandire to hir knees, laughing all the while.

Talis watched, horror-struck, as the black threads appeared once more in Almoris' eyes, wriggling across the surface. More flecked the foam that flowed from hir mouth. Without being aware of falling, Talis found hirself kneeling on the floor of hir cage, clawing at the glass that kept hir from hir spouse's side. Those tiny black threads were leaving Almoris now, flowing towards the shimmering ball in the Prefect's hand.

Almoris gave a huge, gasping breath and then collapsed into a heap as the last of the threads joined with the ball. The Prefect looked up, smiling, and slipped the mysterious ball back into hir robe before sliding the panel closed once more. Talis pushed and slapped at the glass but still it remained, uncracked and immovable.

'What are those things?' Talis demanded. 'What did you do to hir?'

The Prefect looked at Talis, head cocked to the side. 'What do you see?'

'Little black ... threads ... worms ... something. What are they? Did they hurt hir?' Talis rested hir head against the glass and listened to Almoris' wheezing breaths.

'Interesting. Most people can't see them. There are more affinities than we know of,' the Prefect said, not actually answering the question. 'Having an affinity that others don't understand has certain advantages. Like being able to track people without their knowledge.' Ze patted the pocket that the ball was in.

Almoris let out a howl of anguish as hir body arched, hir shoulders pressed against the back wall and heels digging into the floor. It was over as suddenly as it started, and Almoris sagged to the floor, no longer making the same harsh, wheezing sound.

'Almoris,' Talis sobbed. 'My hearts, my soul, please be alright. Almoris.'

'Don't worry, ze isn't dead,' the Prefect said in an obscenely cheerful voice. 'That would be a waste of a perfectly good slave.' Ze glared towards Vinhardt at that last comment.

'Again, I apologise, your grace.' Vinhardt kept hir head bowed as ze spoke. 'It was deeply unfortunate that the other one died. A mistake that will not be repeated.'

'I am sure that it will not,' the Prefect said. 'Otherwise, the person to repeat it may find themselves enslaved, wielder or not.'

Baschal paled and stared at the floor, still gripping Xandire by the arm. Talis looked away from them, hir attention pulled back to Almoris. *Are they talking about Nyqam?* Ze couldn't bring hirself to care about anything other than hir spouse. Ze could see the rise and fall of Almoris' chest and was scared to look away in case the subtle movement stopped.

'Iron-wielders are rare,' the Prefect continued. 'That one would have fetched a good price.'

Iron-wielders. The words pushed themselves through the fog in Talis' mind. Iron-wielders were indeed rare – and Nyqam wasn't one. As far as Talis knew, Nyqam wasn't a wielder at all, just someone who could be persuaded to help them. Batanel. They had to be talking about Batanel.

Ze tore hir eyes away from Almoris and looked at Xandire. The bronze-wielder wore a stricken look that suggested ze had come to the same conclusion.

'Batanel is dead?' Xandire asked, hir voice hoarse.

'Yes,' the Prefect said, looking over Xandire's shoulder at Baschal. 'Despite the fact that I gave clear orders to take hir alive.'

'Then how did you know?' Xandire demanded. 'If Batanel didn't betray us, then who did?'

The Prefect muttered a curse and looked at the ceiling before looking back at hir offspring. 'Have you really failed to work it out?'

'It was Juki,' Talis said, still watching Almoris breathe.

'Vinhardt's pet wood-wielder over there was a trap,' the Prefect said, as if explaining the obvious.

'But Juki didn't know where the exchange was to take place,' Talis said slowly. 'And we weren't followed. We were careful. So how did you find us, if not Batanel?'

'I do believe I have already mentioned that my affinity allows me to track people. A dose in the wood-wielder over there and another in your spouse …' The Prefect was almost giddy over how ze had outsmarted them.

Gradually, rage began to replace fear and sorrow as the dominant emotion in Talis' hearts. Almoris groaned and hir eyelids fluttered. Talis wanted to kill the Prefect for hurting hir spouse, for trying to strangle Xandire, and for all of the slaves that had ever lived under the system the Prefect was complicit with.

'Now, I'd love to stay here and taunt you all evening, but I'm having a dinner tonight for some of the factory owners and Reyam will panic if I'm not back in time.' The Prefect smirked at Xandire. 'Perhaps the offspring that Reyam produces will be more docile than you.'

'How many offspring do you have now?' Xandire asked. 'Seventy isn't it? But only one wielder.'

The Prefect gave Xandire a hard look. Ze had obviously touched on a sore point. *Good,* Talis thought. *Hurt hir any way you can.*

Almoris groaned again and rolled onto hir side then pushed hirself onto hir knees. Ze stopped there, resting on all sixes, taking up most of the floor, head hanging. Something unlocked inside Talis' chest. Ze could breathe again, now that

Almoris was awake. Ze looked around the room, finally able to take everything in. Juki was huddled inside hir cell, crying quietly. Talis could not bring hirself to aim hir anger at the young wood-wielder. Ze had obviously been a slave before coming to them; ze had done what ze had to. Vinhardt stood in the centre of the room, looking a little impatient. Derryl stood behind Xandire, no longer holding hir but clearly ready to intervene should the bronze-wielder try anything. The other slaver stood by the door.

Talis frowned. There was a puddle seeping under the door. Water. Ze glanced up and for the first time heard the rain drumming on the roof. The rain was falling heavily on already water-logged ground. The river that flowed beneath them would be swelling rapidly as storm drains fed water down into its channel and away from the factories with wealthier owners.

'You have two days with them,' the Prefect said, looking at Vinhardt. 'I'll let you know which factory to send them to. Make sure you don't damage them too much to wield their affinity; other than that, do what you like.' Ze started to walk away then stopped beside Xandire. 'This one in particular needs to be taught to obey.'

A high-pitched ringing sound filled Talis's head, making it hard to think. Instinctively, ze reached for the water all around them, but found hirself blocked by the glass. Ze shook hir head and leaned forward, against the wall of hir cell.

Xandire spat straight into the Prefect's face. 'It doesn't matter what you do to us,' ze said, struggling against Derryl who had grabbed hir once more and was pulling hir backwards, away from hir parent. 'Others will replace us. There will always be an underground, helping wielders escape from here.'

The Prefect laughed, a sound of unfettered delight. 'Oh, you poor, simple, child,' ze said at last. 'Haven't you realised? There *is* no underground. You've all been working for me all along.'

Nine

Those words forced themselves through the pain, clearing Almoris' mind. What did the Prefect mean, there was no underground? Surely ze was just taunting them? In the next cell, beyond hir reach, Talis looked shocked.

'You lie,' Almoris said, panting, pulling hirself to hir feet.

'Often,' the Prefect agreed. 'But not this time. Tell them, Vinhardt.'

The slaver stepped forward, closer to the Prefect. 'I am afraid that our illustrious leader is telling the truth. We have been aware of your activities for years.' Ze paused and looked at Xandire. 'Well, not yours. But the other two and your network. You see, we infiltrated the underground before you ever became involved. Replacing one person at a time until the entire network belonged to us.'

'You can't possibly own everyone,' Xandire said, hir voice giving away hir horror.

'Not everyone, no,' the Prefect said. 'But enough of the key elements to be sure of keeping on top of things. All those people you think you've sent to safety over the years? They're slaves in different colonies in Slyvo.'

'That's not true,' Almoris said between gritted teeth. 'You're just trying to hurt us with your lies.'

Almoris could feel the anger rolling off Talis in waves, causing heat to pulse through hir, adding to hir own turmoil.

'You're correct that someone will take over from you. But that someone will belong to me and they will just keep feeding my trade with the other colonies. Through Vinhardt, of course.'

'If all this were true,' Talis said, 'if you really have been running the underground all this time, then why capture us now? What do you gain by removing us?'

'This was never about you,' the Prefect said, shrugging.

'Your friend, Batanel, was not one of ours,' Vinhardt said. 'Ze brought new contacts, ones that we didn't control, and we started losing slaves. We intended to capture hir and leave

72

you both in place.'

'You were supposed to decide that Batanel was a traitor and go back to using your old contacts. Instead, you decided to be heroes.' The Prefect gave Talis and Almoris a disdainful look. 'Still, if you hadn't visited Xandire while I was tracking you, I would never have known of hir involvement. So, I suppose I should thank you for that.'

Almoris' mind was spinning. All of it sounded so horribly plausible. All this time, all of those people that they thought they had helped, really sent off into the hands of the slavers. And Batanel, whose loyalty they had doubted, had been the only one of them actually doing any good. They had to get out of here. They had to make this right somehow.

Almoris' gaze darted about the room, desperately searching for anything they could use to escape. Heat crackled through hir veins, looking for a flame to leap out into, some way to express the fear and rage and powerlessness ze was feeling.

Xandire's knees buckled and Derryl let hir fall to the floor. 'Hyshun, Veritas, Soma … all slaves?'

'As are you, my child,' the Prefect said with a sneer. 'Now, you've made me late. What will Reyam say?' Ze walked towards the door, pulling hir hood up once more.

Xandire buried hir head in hir hands but just as hir parent passed, the bronze-wielder leapt across the floor, colliding with the Prefect at waist height. The two went down in a tangle of limbs. The Prefect yelped while Xandire was hissing and spitting like a trapped feline, struggling on top of hir parent, raining blows down upon the Prefect in a perfect storm of fury. Vinhardt, Derryl and the other slaver looked on in stunned stillness as the Prefect finally seemed to come to terms with what was happening and bucked Xandire off, rolling them both along the floor in front of the cages.

Almoris punched and kicked the glass in front of hir and shouted, a wordless, primal cry that reverberated around the massive room, stunning the slavers out of their stupor. Derryl waded into the fray, pulling at a robe, presumably trying to haul Xandire away. Instead, ze had grabbed the Prefect and received a solid punch to the side of the head that crushed one of hir antennae. Derryl staggered away, hir senses impaired by the injury and stumbled into one of the stands, knocking it and the lamp it held crashing against the front of Almoris' cell, cracking the glass wall of the cell. Not enough to free Almoris, but enough to break the seal.

Almoris' affinity whooshed through hir core, like one of those new gas lamps catching light. The chimney of the lamp had smashed, setting loose the flame. The high emotion of the evening was reducing Almoris' control of hir affinity; if ze did not use it, ze would start to leak. A dangerous possibility when fire was involved. Ze flicked hir fingers at the wooden stand that was still rolling back and forth on the uneven floor. Flames leapt into the air and Almoris' hearts surged with them.

The Prefect had managed to pin Xandire down and had all four hands around hir offspring's neck, bearing down with all hir weight.

Almoris flicked hir fingers again and a ribbon of flame jumped from the burning stand to the hem of the Prefect's cloak. The leader of Cortill screamed like a gull and flapped the cloak, only fanning the flames in hir panic.

Xandire rolled away, gasping and choking until ze came to rest against the front of Talis' cell.

The Prefect hopped from one foot to the other, in a most undignified manner. Almoris concentrated and held the flames at bay.

Xandire pulled hirself to hir feet and slid open the panel at the top of Talis' cell that mirrored the one on Almoris'.

'Your grace!' Vinhardt called, throwing a jug of water towards the Prefect.

Talis raised a hand and stopped the water mid-air, then tossed it back over Vinhardt. The slaver spluttered and Talis made a sound of triumph. Almoris looked at hir spouse and was filled with a surge of fierce pride that Talis had chosen to bond with hir.

Derryl staggered towards the Prefect, unable to get hir bearings with the crushed antennae, and Almoris sent a questing snake of flame into the air between them. The slaver staggered back, whimpering, trapped between the prefect and the wall. The other slaver who had captured them outside, broke and ran for the door. Almoris considered sending a flame after hir but ze was gibbering with fear and did not pose an immediate threat to them.

'Put it out, put it out, put it out,' the Prefect pleaded, staring at the flames that were slowly working their way up hir cloak.

'Let us go first,' Almoris said.

'Of course, of course,' the Prefect said, hir voice taking on a wheedling tone. 'This has all just been a misunderstanding; I wasn't really going to keep you here.'

Almoris hissed through hir teeth and a spark flew onto the Prefect's hand, singeing the skin. The fire-wielder fought back a laugh as the Prefect yelped.

'Vinhardt, unlock the cages!'

The scarred slaver stood looking on, a ponderous expression on hir face. 'I'm afraid I can't do that, your grace,' ze said at last. 'You see, if these were to get away, the whole network would be lost. Not to mention the unrest it could cause amongst the other slaves if word got out.'

'What are you talking about?' the Prefect demanded. 'I'm on *fire*. Of course, we're going to co-operate!'

'But you see, *I'm* not on fire. And I'm the one with the keys,' Vinhardt said, thoughtfully jangling the keys as if to remind everyone who had the power in the room. 'I don't believe they will allow you to die but, if they do, they have lost their bargaining power and I have lost only a master.'

'You will pay for this, you putrescent pustule,' the Prefect growled, for a moment seeming to forget the flames in hir anger at Vinhardt.

'What makes you think I won't send the flame for you?' Almoris asked softly.

'Your spouse has already made sure that I am quite soaked,' Vinhardt answered with a smirk. 'I do not believe that wet cloth burns well.'

Talis made a beckoning gesture with hir fingers and droplet by droplet, the water freed itself from Vinhardt's clothing and danced through the air to float in front of the cells.

'Better, my love?' Talis asked.

Almoris grinned. 'Perfect.' Ze flicked a tongue of flame from the Prefect to Vinhardt and laughed a harsh, barking laugh as it caught the slaver's sleeve. Ze concentrated, controlling both flames, keeping either from badly burning the people they were threatening. There was, however, only so long that ze could contain the fire this way. Sooner or later, it would spread or die out. They needed to get out of these cells before either of those things happened.

'Give the keys to Xandire,' Almoris said, allowing the flames to spread a little further up the respective pieces of clothing, letting the heat build and break through enough to cause some pain as an incentive for the them to do as they were instructed.

Vinhardt was holding hir burning sleeve as far away from hir body as ze could reach. Wordlessly, ze dropped the keys onto the floor and kicked them towards Xandire.

'Talis, then Juki, then me,' Almoris said to Xandire, still watching Vinhardt and the Prefect.

Xandire unlocked Talis's cell and was halfway across the room to Juki's by the time Talis swung the heavy door open and stepped out, into a puddle. The water that was seeping under the door raced towards the water-wielder, gathering close to hir, awaiting instructions.

Xandire seemed to be struggling with Juki. Almoris flicked hir eyes in that direction as Talis went over to help. Juki appeared to be in shock. Xandire was half-carrying hir out of the cell, grunting with the weight. Talis took over and supported the younger wielder while Xandire hurried back over with the keys.

Almoris sent the flames flaring up into the air around both the Prefect and Vinhardt as ze carefully stepped out of the cell. Derryl whimpered and staggered towards the door. Almoris shared a glance with Talis then let the injured slaver go.

'Put these flames out,' the Prefect begged. 'Do what you like with Vinhardt. Ze's the one who's really in charge. I'm just a poor politician who got caught up in something I didn't understand. You can let me go; I won't be any danger to you.'

'What will we do with them?' Almoris asked Talis as ze approached with Juki. 'I can't leave them burning but if I put the flames out now, there's nothing to stop them coming after us.'

'Get into the cell,' Talis said, nodding towards the cell that Almoris had recently vacated.

'You can't put me in there,' the Prefect objected. 'I'm the most important person in this colony. I could be a good friend to you.'

'Both of you,' Almoris said, letting the flames spread a little. 'Into the cells, now.'

Vinhardt almost sprinted for the cell, the flames lapping at hir elbow. The Prefect stood staring between Almoris and the glass box. Almoris flicked hir fingers and the trousers the politician wore beneath hir cloak caught fire, the flames climbing hir leg quickly. The Prefect gave a little scream and dived into the cell, pulling the door closed behind hir.

Xandire quickly locked both doors and opened the panel on the cell that Almoris had been in, allowing hir to keep controlling the flame, then threw the key to the other end of the large room.

The fire was hungry and pulled at Almoris' control. Soon, it would break free and neither of these parasites would be safe.

'Talis, some help please,' Almoris said in a low voice, sweat popping out on hir forehead.

Talis pulled the water on the floor up into a wave that ze sent in a powerful stream through the open panels on each cell with enough force to knock them both from their feet. Then ze called the water back, leaving them both wet and spluttering.

'Let's go,' ze said, turning towards Almoris and reaching out one of the hands not busy supporting Juki.

'This isn't over, you know,' the Prefect growled, getting to hir feet. 'I will hunt you down and make you pay for this. You'll wish you had been auctioned to one of the factories.'

'Ignore hir,' Almoris said, taking Talis's hand.

'Xandire, there is nowhere you can hide from me. You know I have the money and connections to find you, wherever you run.'

Xandire looked pale but determined. 'I'll make sure that the whole of Slyvo knows what you've been doing. That you've been falsely accusing wielders of crimes they did not commit so that you could enslave them and make your friends rich.'

'You are such a fool, child.' The Prefect glared at Xandire

through the glass. 'The people with the power to stop me are the ones who are benefitting from what we do. No-one cares what happens to wielders unless it directly affects them.'

Talis gripped Almoris' hand so tightly that ze was crushing it. 'Ze's right,' the water-wielder said. 'We can get away, but we can't stop them.'

Water splashed up Almoris' leg and ze looked down, surprised to see that the entire floor was covered now. The noise of the rain drumming on the roof grew suddenly louder, more forceful. In hir anger, Talis was affecting all of the water around them, pulling it towards hirself.

The walls, already weakened by the damp and rot that had set into them years before they had ever come here, began to groan as Talis' power pulled the moisture from their very core. The water on the floor was rising. Now it was half-way up Almoris' shin.

'Time to go, my love,' Almoris said, tugging at hir spouse's arm.

'We can't just leave them. They have to pay for what they've done. How many lives have been ruined because of their greed?'

The water on the floor was surging in choppy waves, reacting to Talis' anger. Almoris looked at the two slavers in the cage. The Prefect was smirking at them, still living in the confidence that hir money and power brought. Still not in fear, despite the circumstances. Vinhardt looked a bit more concerned but not truly worried.

'Talis, Juki needs help. We have to get hir somewhere safe and warm.' Almoris knew that the best way to bring Talis back to hirself was to trigger hir need to care for people. Ze was incapable of turning hir back on someone who needed help.

Talis stared at the two slavers a moment longer, the need for revenge warring with the need to get away with Juki. Ze strode to the cell, the water parting to let hir pass.

'I expect both of you to get out of Cortill,' Talis said, matter-of-factly. 'If you stay here, if you go back to your old ways, I will come for you. There won't be any warning. You'll just find yourself drowning someday.'

The walls groaned again, and water surged around them.

Almoris half-lifted, half-dragged Juki while Xandire grabbed Talis and dragged hir towards the door. A sharp cracking noise filled the space and a chunk of wall splashed down into the water. Vinhardt started to panic.

'You can't just leave us here,' ze shouted slamming hir hands into the wall. 'This building could collapse!'

Almoris only looked back to make sure that Talis and Xandire were behind hir. The four of them reached the door as a piece of the roof fell into the middle of the room, allowing the rain to pound down inside the building.

'Let us out!' Vinhardt cried. 'Let us out!'

'Xandire, get back here,' the Prefect shouted, adopting the stern tone of a parent dealing with an unruly child.

Almoris pulled the door open and stepped back, letting Xandire and Talis pass. Ze glanced back at the cell to see Vinhardt scrabbling at the panel opening, which was barely more than a hands-width.

'This is all your fault,' ze was screaming at the Prefect.

Almoris smiled as ze walked outside into the rain and pulled the door closed behind hir.

The gate lay open at the end of the path and the four of them waded through puddles, slipping and sliding in the mud they created, until they reached the road. There they stopped and looked back at the building. Talis held out all four arms and roared to the sky. The rain flew away from them, straight at the building, while water flowed from the ground. More creaks and groans sounded from the walls and a great crack ripped up the side of the building they faced.

It seemed to Almoris later that everything happened in slow motion then. The walls began to lean inwards, crashes and splashes echoed across the night. The clang of something hard hitting against metal reached hir ears and then the steady rumble of the building collapsing drowned out all other noise. Mostly what Almoris remembered about that moment was Talis, standing with hir arms raised, head tipped back to face the sky, wind whipping through hir hair. Ze looked like a deity and Almoris wanted nothing more than to worship at hir feet.

Ten

The sun beat down on Talis' back as the ship docked in Thespa, the main port in Akros. The wood creaked beneath hir feet. Ze would be glad to be on land once more. Their voyage had been smooth for the most part but Talis had been overcome by a restlessness that could not be walked off while on the ship. Ze needed to wander freely, the world at hir feet.

'At last,' Almoris said, stepping up beside hir and putting a hand on hir shoulder. 'I was starting to think we would never get here.'

Talis rested hir cheek against Almoris' hand and smiled. After that night, ze had worried that Almoris would leave, that ze would no longer be able to love hir after what ze had done. Hir actions had caused the deaths of Vinhardt and the Prefect, and justified or not, it had changed hir. There had been no need to worry.

Almoris had held hir in the night when ze woke up screaming from dreams of the cells, treating hir gently but not fearfully. When Xandire had arranged passage to Akros, Talis had made it clear that Almoris could go alone, that ze could be free, if that was hir desire. Almoris had said that if ze could choose to bond again tomorrow, ze would still choose Talis. So, they had set off on this adventure together.

Juki joined them as they made their way down the gang plank and onto the pier. The young wood-wielder had begun to recover when they were underway, and they had managed to get some of hir story.

Juki had not been kicked out by hir nest-guardian as ze first told Talis. When ze had begun to display an affinity, the nest-guardian had sold the child to Vinhardt, who had apparently thought hir rather sweet and kept hir as a personal slave rather than sell hir on. Ze had been with Vinhardt for two years before the slaver decided to use hir to trap Batanel.

They had questioned hir extensively about their friend, in the hope that the iron-wielder was not really dead, that ze had somehow escaped. Juki didn't know anything other than what Vinhardt had told them.

'Excuse me, are you Talis Water Dancer?' a young Akrian person said.

'Yes,' Talis answered warily. It still seemed so strange to have total strangers aware of hir affinity, to not have to hide anymore.

'I am Perun,' the young person said, pushing black hair out of hir eyes and giving a little half-bow. 'Xandire has made arrangements for you. I am to escort you to your lodgings and see that you have everything you need, then first thing tomorrow, I will take you on a tour of the available properties that suit your needs. Xandire said that you would be establishing a boarding house for wielders?'

'That is correct,' Talis said, smiling.

'I've found three buildings that I think may meet your needs,' Perun said, leading the way through the throng of people at the docks and talking over hir shoulder.

Talis took a deep breath, straightened hir back, lifted hir antennae and followed.

The sun was high in the sky when they approached the final building that Perun had located for them. This one was on the outskirts of Thespa, where it seemed that the wealthier Akrians lived, rather than in the centre of the colony as they did in Slyvo. Perun had offered to hire a palanquin but Talis had insisted on walking and hir muscles had a pleasant ache after the confines of the ship.

Life was very different here and would take some getting used to. Talis and Almoris had woken to find their room filled with small, brightly-coloured birds who had found their way in through the open shutters and were putting on an aerial display above the bed, having eaten from the tray of fruit that had been left out the night before. It had taken quite some time to chase them all from the room and by the time the shutters were closed, they were sweating and laughing.

The building they approached now was at the end of a quiet, dusty street and sat in large grounds, behind a wall of white stone. Two large, iron gates barred the way. Talis turned to Perun to ask if ze had key when Almoris gasped and gripped hir arm.

'Talis, look!'

Talis looked back in time to see the gates swing open with no apparent cause. Almost as if an iron-wielder had opened them. A moment later, hir antennae tingled with a familiar vibration and ze ran into the grounds, filled with joy.

The End

Acknowledgements

It's odd, but I find these harder to do than the initial writing of the book. There are so many people that I am grateful to, so many people who touch my work and my life. It seems impossible to name each one and to show the depth of my gratitude.

Once more, I owe my thanks to Adele for taking on another of my odd little novellas. Fox Spirit really are Fearless Genre Warriors and I'm very proud to call myself skulk. Thank you to Darren Pulsford for editing and to the rest of the team who bring this book to you.

My thanks also go to Kate Coe who provided a first edit on this before it was with Adele and who remained a champion of the story throughout its journey.

Lee Fletcher was one of my early readers and provided invaluable feedback. It really wouldn't be the same story without them.

As always, my mum read an early draft and helped me talk through which bits were working and where to tweak. She's also asked for a sequel so if I get around to it, you'll have her to thank/blame as you see fit.

Thank you to my writing friends who either looked at sections of this, let me talk through the idea and/or cheered me on at submission time. This includes but is not limited to: Mike Brooks, Stewart Hotston, Phil Lunt, Pete McLean, Diane McLean, Natalie Fergie and Tabatha Stirling.

Lastly, thank you to Brian. None of my books would exist without his support.

Thank you for buying this Fox Spirit Book.
We hope you enjoyed it.

Fox Spirit believes that day to day life lacks a few things. We need the fantastic, the magical, the mischievous and even a touch of the horrific to stave off the banal and humdrum. Let the skulk bring you stories full of wonder and mischief delivered with a sharp bite.

Join the Skulk at foxspirit.co.uk